'Bout Them Angels

H. Dietrich Brinkmeyer

AmErica House
Baltimore

© 2001 by H. Dietrich Brinkmeyer.

First printing

ISBN: 1-58851-245-2
PUBLISHED BY AMERICA HOUSE BOOK
PUBLISHERS
www.publishamerica.com
Baltimore

Printed in the United States of America

In addition to my wife I would like to acknowledge help from some real angels who have whispered in my ear and pushed me in the right direction all my life, even with this book. To these angels - I say thank you.

Special thanks to Bill and Linda Czech and Jade Bourke.

To—

Laurel—

"May the Angels watch over you!"

H. Dietrich Brinkmeyer

2/4/02

Part I

Evolution of Andrew Brown

Chapter 1
Angels

Well, there they are – "Angels." We'll call them angels anyway. I know that's the best term you understand. You see, they're timeless. This gets complicated. After all, there is no time here. It's endless – has no beginning – stands still. Oh, just accept it for now.

About these "Angels" – they are not human. They are part of this "real world." Not earth. They are part of that great central power. Definitely different from the part that split off at a different "time." One thing they do is help people who are going through the earth experience by communication with them. Note that the communication here is greater than that known on earth – so for anyway. They do not use vocal chords and ears. They don't have any. First of all the transfer of information is instantaneous and complete. It not only contains the equivalent of sound, sight and feeling but also the complete emotion and – how can I "say" it – the transfer of the complete experience.

Example: If you went on a trip for a month and visited many places, you could transfer the whole experience to someone in an instant, including all you see, feel emotionally, even your thoughts. All of this would be more than we can accomplish here with earth methods. The method that Angels use to communicate is a way unknown to us completely. To understand their communication, it must be interpreted for us. It would be impossible to completely understand if it were not. Unfortunately, some is lost in the translation. But the only thing we can do is to relate it as close as possible. Further, the communication here and the attempt with earth people is in many different forms. "Angels" do communicate and try to influence the ways of life on earth. We want to look at some of it here and try to understand. Let us go now to the "Angels" and "listen" in as they work with and observe the earth happenings.

Angels

"Is this the place? Rather small."

"Yes, this is it. 'Earth' as they call it. One of the growth and experience places – small as it is. The ones going through it see it as rather large and long, to them and an 'all there is' world in itself. That is of course because they are encased in a time sort of thing and with no real experience with the outer world."

"There are several here we are to help. They come together later and reinforce each other. There is the one called Brown, Andrew Brown. But before we get to him we must follow their "time" procedure and respond to a rather strong call for help and one that must be completed so the descendants will even be around to help. It is a rather poor group, by earth's standards, actually called slaves."

"They do, however, possess a treasure few even know about."

"I know. Let us go now. We will start from the beginning with Brown later, and join with others as we go. Some of our aids are actually there on earth, as physical beings. In that way they become *fully* involved in the earth life. Even to the point of making mistakes."

"Yes, help comes from many sources. It certainly helps when they place their minds in the center position so they can communicate."

"Sadly, some never even try or do not get past the very beginning position of only asking for things, not realizing what vast communication could be achieved even at the earth level."

8

"And they do need the help, since some rather strong forces are at work from the negative side."

"True. Let us slow to *their* level and observe the happenings at this time."

***

"Carolina? What is Carolina?"

"South Carolina actually. Come, we are needed.

***

"'Saiha! 'Saiha! Please, I need your help. Can you get me in to see Mista Calab? 'Saiha, my Amy is bad sick. I've done everything I know. She's burning up and she's talk'un outta her head. I gotta get a doctor some way and I know no doctor gonna come down here. But, maybe if Mista Calab call him–"

"Woman, you know Mr. Calab don't talk to slaves and he sure ain't go'na call no Doctor."

"I got to do sumthun. I'm afraid she's gonna die if'n I don't. She's all I got! I–"

"Isaiah! What's all that racket out there. Who's that woman and what's she do'un in here?"

"Name's Miss Maudy, she from the cabins down there. Says her little child is bad sick - need a doctor. Want's me to ask you if'n you'd call one. I told her–"

"You tell her to get that old women that takes care of sick folks down there. She'll take care of what ever needs to be done. I suppose she wants me to pay the doctor bill too, huh?"

"She never said nothing 'bout that Sir. But they ain't got no money."

"I know they ain't. An' you tell her to quit com'un up here - ya hear?"

"Yes sir, I hear."

***

"Miss Maudy, Mister Calab said for you to get old Emma Mae. He said she could take care of what ever needs to be."

"I talked to her already. Amy needs a doctor, a real doctor. Please Isaiah, I–"

"Look woman, don't go try'un to get me into no trouble with Mr. Calab. He done said "no" and that's it. You know that. Now go on back and get Emma Mae and do the best you can."

***

Maudy did just that. She told Emma Mae and Emma Mae had already told most of the folks on "the row." Soon people began to come to Maudy's cabin. Some, mostly the women went inside and talked to Maudy. They brought things to eat, blankets and anything else they could think of to help. The men stayed outside, mostly. Some built a fire and they cooked some broth. Special kind. They talked together about what they could do to help Maudy and her daughter. Someone brought a pillow so Maudy could put it behind her head while she sat beside little Amy. Then a strange thing seemed to be developing. Folks gathered around Maudy's cabin. There were so many of them there was a circle all the way around. More came.

Soon you could hear humming like – and every now and then some singing. Now and then someone just worded a prayer. And everyone would say, "Amen." Two or three women kinda stayed close to Maudy and tried to provide what ever she needed or wanted. What ever it was and what ever they could do. The folks stayed all night, most still standing. They kept singing quietly and sorta swaying back and forth. Every now and then one of the women would come to the door and give a request for something and someone would go and get it or they'd give a report on Amy's progress. They all knew they had to go back into the fields in the morning. No one left. When the dawn came up they were still there.

Then, suddenly, one of the women came to the door and said, "Her fever's broke!"

Lots of "Amens" and even "Hallelujahs" could be heard - in a solemn sort of way. Slowly the group of people around the small cabin begin to leave and go back to their own places and prepare for another day's work. In the days that passed Amy recovered completely.

***

Old Calab McDanielson, the plantation owner was as hard a man as they come. His wife had left him years ago and his two children also had moved away. For years he had been living by himself. The years took its toll on him and he was often sick. His servant, Isaiah, was the only one he ever confided in and did his bidding seven days a week twenty-four hours a day. Isaiah was too old and crippled up to do any work in the field. He figured that was the only way he could survive.

Old Mister McDanielson grew sick again. Worse than ever before. He had Isaiah call the doctor many times but it had become futile.

"Isaiah! Come here!"

"Yes sir, Mr. Calab, what can I get you, Mr. Calab?"

"You know – that woman – Maudy, that was here once – had that kid that was sick?"

"Yes sir."

"Fetch her! Tell her – to come here – right in here – alone! Go on!"

"Bring her here. Yes sir. I'm go'un."

"Miss Maudy, Miss Maudy! You in there?"

"I'm right here. You don't need to holler. What's the matter?"

"Miss Maudy, Mr. Calab say he want you to come to him – right there in his room. He's sick. I think he's outta his head, but he say to bring you, so you better come."

"What ever for?"

"Don't know. Just come on. He's bad sick you know."

"He's bad sick and he wants to see me. You sure 'Saiha?"

"Yeah, I'm sure and he say come alone. So you come along now."

***

11

"Mr. Calab? It's Maudy! Maudy, the one that had the child that was sick."

"I know which Maudy it is. Sit down."

"Isaiah said you wanted to see me. I –"

"Yes I sent for you. Sit down there. You know, I'm very ill. I guess there isn't much to do for me anymore – or they would do it. Miss Maudy – you hear me?"

"Yes sir, I hear you."

"I don't want to die this way. There's nothing, nor no one. The doctors can do nothing, and my family's gone. I don't want this. But don't seem to be anything I can do about it."

"What can I do fer you, Mr. Calab. Can I fetch you a cup of water?"

"No. I know I turned you away when you asked me for help – a while back. I have lived to regret that. But I didn't help you none –."

"It all turned out all right, Mr. Calab."

"I know. You turned to the only thing you had. I guess. You didn't get anything from me. I have nothing left to turn to. You have something – that I don't have and don't understand. I want to know how I can get what you have. You know – what I mean?"

"I'm not sure Mr. Calab, sir. We just do the best we can and when things is beyond us, well, we comes to the Good Lord. Is that what you mean Mr. Calab?"

"I suppose. I didn't help *you*. Will He help me?"

"They say, He helps them that is really sorry and ask for Him to help them. I think that's up to you and o 'course – the Good Lord. But I think He helps anybody that really asks Him. I heard the preacher say that He even forgave that man that was on the cross beside Him."

"Miss Maudy – Miss Maudy – what do I do?"

"Mr. Calab, if I was you, I'd just lay back and rest myself and think about all that's bother'un me. You can't go undo'un anything nor fix'un nothing. You just ask the Lord to come to you - He will, and you ask Him to forgive you – and I think He'll do that too. Then you just rest. I'll be here if you need anything. You just rest."

***

"Laudy – Miss Maudy! I hear ole Mr. Calab died in his sleep last night and you was with him. Is that a fact?"

"Yes he did. Was dead this morning anyway. Strange thing. All the years I knowed ole Mr. Calab I never seen him smile. But he had a smile on his face this morning – an' him be'un sick and all.

Strange!"

Angels

"Yes, strange to people of earth I suppose. But stranger things have happened and still do."

***

"We must get back to the one called Brown. He is not going very far if we don't help him now! He has great potential. We cannot lose him in this earth picture just now."

"Oh, these earth happenings! We must become involved. Observe!"

The Barn
(Much time has passed)

When Andrew Brown was just a boy, six years old, he sometimes went with his uncle who worked part time at a neighboring farm. Andrew's mother was ill and his father was working one day, so Andrew went with his uncle to the farm while they baled and stored hay.

It was a typical mid-west farm, spread out all over and a barn much bigger than the house. But that was the usual way with mid-west farms. After all, the barn was necessary for

making a living. The house was just a place to sleep and eat –
ask any mid-west farmer.

The barn, of course, was a big red one with a hayloft above
and a place for the cows below. There was always a pile of hay
down below and Andrew liked to play in it.

This particular day he was doing the same and making little
piles of hay and moving them around with a small cart his
uncle had given him. He imagined houses and roads and all
sorts of things in that pile of hay.

His attention was completely in the make-believe setting of
the hay and cart, ignoring altogether the loading operation
going on above him. His uncle and the farmer were moving
bales of hay from the truck to the loft above and stacking them
for winter.

Suddenly, he heard a loud voice. "Andrew, get up – get out
of here quick! Andrew, get up – get out of here quick!"

It so startled Andrew that he got up and got out of there –
quick!

When he did, four large bales of hay fell right where he was
playing and smashed his wooden cart. Surely, if he had not
moved they would have smashed him, too. His uncle said they
were large alfalfa bales, over a hundred pounds apiece.

Needless to say, it made quite an impression on Andrew. He
said the voice was a women. Sounded something like his
mother.

He thought about it quite a bit, long after it happened, and
I think it's still tucked away in his memory somewhere yet
today.

The "voice," of course, saved Andrew's life.

Angels

This is a very rare type of communication. It does happen.
Far more often the communication is even unknown by the
receiver.

"Our mission here is to work with earth-people. Andrew Brown is one. It would have stopped here if no extreme means were applied."

"I understand you tried to get a message to him mentally, telling him to do something else – or to his uncle – conditions were not in line. Usually, humans are used to influence humans. The other method was necessary here."

"We will continue now, of course, to follow Andrew through this earth experience."

The Party
(Much later)

"Well, good morning Mrs. Brown. How you feeling this morn'un?"

"Mrs. Brown?! Well honey, Mrs. Brown is do'un just fine...an' how's Mrs. Wills do'un?"

"Oh I'm enjoy'un poor health, thank you...ha. Say I hear you're have'un a do'uns at your place tonight. Can anybody come? Even though they ain't got no money?"

"Heh, heh – if we left out them that ain't got no money we wouldn't have much of a party. I didn't think I had to send out invites. You and Ward come on. I was kinda count'un on him bringing his banjo and pick'un. Ya hear?"

"We be there. He's go'un down to the hole after work. If he catches anything, we'll bring some fish."

"That'd be fine. We got some, but you can't never have too much. Rev. Johnson go'un to be there...he's a big fish eater."

"Heh, heh...yeah...that's true. All right now...we'll see you tonight."

"We be look'un for you."

***

Parties at the Brown house were a thing to behold. Things like that don't happen anymore. The house wasn't very large, but then they didn't have a lot of furniture so it was easy to move it back and leave room to dance. Some even danced outside in the summer.

That night, people brought what they had and several people just started fix'un things and cooking fish over an open fire in back. Whole families came...even kids. When the little ones fell asleep they just put them to bed somewhere. After Rev. Johnson got his fill of fish...he usually led the group in some songs. Everybody sang. Sounded pretty good sometimes. Seemed odd, how sometimes, someone would just break out into a solo. Just like as if they rehearsed it. Course they didn't. When Rev. Johnson left, people usually started dancing, and it went on till they decided to quit.

***

"Andrew! Come on out here. You been sit'un there like a bump on a log all evening ..."

"A ... mama ..."

"I know...you don't want to dance with your mama. Well, you just come on anyway. Willie play a slow one."

"Mama ..."

"Now you just hush...you're do'un just fine. - You know, your father and I used to dance to this...some time ago. Since you're the man of the house now, you can just take over and treat your ole mama to a dance now and again. Look at Mary Ann. She's dance'un with her uncle."

Andrew "broke the ice" slowly, but after a while, was dancing with everybody...almost. Such parties had been a common thing at the Brown's in the past, before Andrew's father got killed in an accident working for the barge line. It had been quite a while since the last one, so Mrs. Brown decided it was time to do it again. So she did. Everyone helped.

There were others, and Andrew remembered these times at home as the good life he hoped to find and live with the rest of his life.

16

Angels

"It's these 'real' experiences in any person's life, including Andrew's, that help support them later and give them some real memories to remind them of the genuine good times that can be enjoyed. We must help Andrew keep these and use them to guide him in the future."

B.B. Beach
(Later - 1937)

"Mama, mama - this you wash'un day? I got the wood. It's stacked by the back door. Bo and I are go'un to the river. We might stay all night. Can I have a potato?"

"You got enough? There's three of us wash'un, you know."

"Yes, um. It's clean up to the window."

"Well, go on. - Yes you can have a potato. Just one – ya hear? You and Bo mind that river now. It gets somebody nearly every year. Andrew, bring me home some corn. But be careful."

"Yes'um, we will!"

***

Well, Bo's still got a daddy work'un. Maybe he can afford to get a can of beans. One time he got two.

Aw - oh - his mama's got him sweep'un. I hope that don't mean he has to stay and help clean the house.

"Bo - hey, you go'un today?"

"Oh hi Drew. Didn't see you. I gotta sweep and take out that trash in the back. C'mon help me. I gotta get it done before my mama gets back....She wants me to do some other stuff. And she said I couldn't have noth'un. C'mon, let's get it done and get out of here."

"OK - let's go – got the beans?"

"I got'um. Get outta here!"

"We go'un to that place you told me – out on that bar?"

"Yeah, best place around here."

I ain't never been there before. You said it's a mean swim?"

"Aw, it's noth'un. You just got to do it right. I'll show ya."

"A'right. Hey, let's cut across the tracks and through ole Cotter Field."

"OK. Nobody's play'un baseball there today, I guess. Your brother still play with that 'Cats' team? What's his name?"

"Yeah, the Black Cats. They call him Radio."

"Radio?"

"A - huh. He's got one. I was over there the other day and he was listen'un to something from Nashville, Tenn. and New York City."

"Man, how can he afford something like that?"

"Well, he sorta – found it."

"Oh. Hey we want to go over to 21st street, by the white folks houses, and go right straight down to the river."

"Where do we go to get the corn?"

"Other side of the levee. I mean, bunches of it. Some old white peck owns it and he gets hot sometimes and gets his shotgun out. But don't worry. We'll just grab some and hit it for the river."

"What 'da we do with it then?"

"Well we don't want to get too much. Only what we can eat over there. We'll get some to take home later. And we have to stick 'em in our pants for the swim over, so don't take too many."

"OK."

"A, you'll be see'un it in just a minute when we get to the top of the levee."

"Aw, crips Drew. There's miles of it."

"I know. Come on, we just got to get to the end here and grab some and beat it to the river. Don't mess around. Ya hear?"

"I hear. I hear."

"Just grab a couple and let's get...."

"GET OUT OF THERE - YOU BLACK....!"

-------- BLAM!!

"Holy Moses - Drew, he's shoot'un!"

"I hear. Don't run down the row. Cut through so he can't see you so easy. Head for the river. And don't say no more. - Go!"

-------- BLAM!!

"Drew - he's in that pickup!"

"I know - run - and shut up."

***

"Bo - duck down in these bushes. He can't see us and he sure ain't coming down in here."

"I'm duck'un – I'm duck'un. You didn't tell me that ole man had a shotgun."

"Aw, sure I did. They all got'em. Forget it. He ain't go'un to chase us anymore over a couple a ears of corn. You get some?"

"I got three. You said we couldn't swim with too many."

"That'll do. We'll set a throw line. Maybe catch us an ole 'cat' or two. We'll do all right."

"Drew! Drew!! That's a snake. Look out! I'm gett'un out of here."

"Oh, a moccasin! Don't run. Rock'em. He's more 'fraid of you than you are a him."

"Oh, no, he ain't."

"He's gone. He crawled down to the river. He's gone."

"An' we go'na swim in that water...?"

"He's gone I tell you. Half way down to the Point by now."

***

"Well, let's move on up a bit. We got to get out on the edge of that rip rap stick'un out. But we got to get ready before we go out on it. It's a little shaky."

"What da ya mean, get ready?!"

"Well, you gotta tie your shoe strings together and let'em hang down the back of your neck. Tie'em tight so's they won't

19

come undone but long enough to go around your neck and hang down your back. Don't want to lose 'em when you swim."

"I ain't go'un."

"Come on, Bo. I didn't think you'd turn around on me."

"Well, what else we got a do?"

"Stick your bean can in your back pocket. It'll go. Shove it in there good. Wait a minute – you got a tie you shoes together in the back or you'll lose 'em."

"I don't know 'bout this."

"C'mon, I don't need no chicken."

"I ain't chicken! What you do'un now?"

"I got the tater in my pocket and we have to have some matches to start a fire. I know there's only one way to keep them dry - with paper matches anyway. You got to stick 'em in your mouth and keep you mouth shut when you're swim'un. They don't taste very good so I tear off the end ones on both sides so I don't touch the matches much with my mouth. Got your corn tight so they don't come out?"

"I guess so. Ever lose any?"

"At first. Now look, we got to jump in here and swim like the devil for that part stick'un out over there. See this cross current? Well it'll take you to New Orleans if you let it. You got a get past it fast and into that back water over there. Then you can just swim easy the rest of the way to the bar. Got it?"

"You go first."

"I'll go first, but don't forget what I told you!"

"Is there any other way to get over there?"

"No, no! C'mon. Watch me and do just like I do. But you gotta give it ever thing you got at first."

***

Um, um, this baby's move'un today. Um, the corn's slip'un. Gotta stop that. I lost a little ground. Gotta move – oh, I think I'm go'na make it. Aw, my toe hit the sand. Now, come on Bo!

"Go Bo go! C'mon!"

Aw, man he's lose'un ground. He's gotta get by that center.
"Andrew! Andrew! ANDREW!! Help - HELP! I......"
Aw, man I can't go back in that water! I GOTTA. I GOTTA.
Andrew is tired like he's never been before, but one look at
Bo and he knows if he doesn't get him out of that river – quick
– he may never see him again. That ole river's mean and swift.
Andrew starts running down the edge of the sand bar as fast
and as far as he can. Then he realizes he has to hit the water.
He thought he was swimming as fast as he could, swimming
over. Somehow he finds the energy to give it even more. He
has to if he is going to make it to Bo. Andrew does just that –
makes it to Bo. He spins him half way around and puts his arm
over one shoulder, around and under the other arm. He tells Bo
to kick and they start a very slow and very agonizing swim to
the sandy shore. Andrew swallows a lot of water. Just before
they get to where they can stand, Andrew throws up. A few
more painful strokes and their feet feel the sand. They both fall
down. Get up again and fall and stumble their way to the dry
sand. Both lay flat on their backs and do nothing for quite some
time.

"Bo! You all right?"
"I don't know what I am right now. But I do know I
wouldn't be noth'un and I wouldn't be here if you hadn't pulled
me out of that mess. I owe you Drew – a bunch."
"I had to do it. After all you had the bean can!"
"Bean can, yeah. Well long as we're here, might as well
enjoy it. I sure ain't go'un to swim back, at least not right
now."
"Just take it easy and let's walk back and go over to the
other side. Nice over there."
"I saw my sick mama there for a minute. I thought I was
go'un for a river ride."
"You did it. You did good. C'mon let's go over there."
"Hey, this is the good stuff. Looks just like Hawaii."
"Shhh. What you know about Hawaii?"

"Oh I used to go there all the time. All them hula girls used to dance for me."

"A - huh! Well come on, you big world traveler, let's go build a fire on this ole Mississippi beach."

"I though this was 'Bare But Beach?'"

"It is. C'mon. Stink'un matches are wet. Can't understand it. I guess they'll dry out if they sit here in the sun a couple hours. C'mon. Let's go down over there – take a little swim."

"Yeah, that's all I need. I'm com'un."

***

"When you was in Hawaii, I was in Africa swing'un on a grape vine. Want to see how I do it?"

"Oh, I was just kidd'un about Hawaii. But I know you can't swing on no grape vine."

"No. I'm real up. Look here, see all that mess hanging down from the trees? And see how that one big piece goes down to the ground? Well, you got your knife?"

"Yeah."

"Well bring it over. If we cut that bugger off just above the ground and clear out a little of that crap above we got us a swing – c'mon help me."

"Hey, this things almost as tough as a tree trunk."

"I know. Keep cut'un."

"There, now we got it. Look, see that sand hump. Pull that sucker back and stand there. I bet you can swing right out over the river!"

"You go ahead. I'm watch'un."

"I'm on it. I'm on it. Watch out."

PLOP-

"Hey! Hey! What's a matter Tarzan? You miss the river?"

"Aw, shut up. You just watch this time."

After several attempts and a little adjustment, Bo and Andrew both become expert "Tarzans" and spend hours swinging out over the river and dropping in the water.

"Hey, Bo let's go check those matches. If they're dry, lets build a fire and put out a throw line. Aw, yeah, they dry. Pick up all this little crap you can. Get the dry stuff. Then when it gets go'un we can just pile on some big 'uns.. . . Now, we got us a fire here. Get your bean can an' be sure you punch a hole in it. And set it close to the fire."

"What you go'un a do, suck the juice outta that thing?"

"No, man. Don't you know if that thing gets too hot it'll blow and you'll get hot beans all over you? They burn."

"That so?"

"Yeah, that's so. Look you fix the bean can and I'll fix this potato. An' nen get the corn and put 'em right by the fire. We can push 'em in closer later."

"What you go'un to do with that tator?"

"Pack this ole sticky gumbo all around it. An' pack it good...so's it won't burn when it's by the fire."

"Ain't cha go'un a eat it?"

"Sure, sure. This just keeps it from burn'un. It comes off. - But still cooks it good."

"OK."

"Now, let me find a good rock. I brought my string and hook. Gotta find one I can tie on for a sinker so's it won't come off. Then all I gotta do is dig a worm or two and chunk it in the river - and wait."

"You ever catch anything?"

"Sometimes. Just leave it and we'll check it later."

"That's OK with me."

Bo and Andrew spend the rest of the day "swinging on a grapevine" and floating down to the end of the sand bar and walking back.

***

"Well, go'un a be dark soon. When do we eat?"

"Let's go check the line and fix it."

"Hey, Drew! Look, you got someth'un on that crazy line."

"Yeah, pull her in."

"I don't see nothing flopp'un around."

"Cat. He down there."

"I don't believe it. Look at that sucker!"

"Yeah, OK We got him. Hit him on the head with that rock. Hard!"

"I thought I did."

"OK, OK, he's dead."

"Now we'll just skin him, cut him, peel out his backbone and then hang him on a stick by the fire and man - m - m - we'll have us a corn, beans, and catfish dinner."

"Sounds good, Drew. Sounds good. This is the way it used to be in Hawaii. Naw you know I was fibb'un about Hawaii. I never really been there."

"That so. I thought that's where you got that good look'un tan. Heh, heh."

"No, no, really I didn't go to Hawaii. It was Jamaica!"

"Oh Bo, you full of it!"

"Aw, yeah. I used to sit there by the ocean and smoke them big cigars."

"Yeah, I suppose you danced with them good look'un women in Jamaica too. Huh?"

"Sure man, I had 'em wait'un on me...bring'un me drinks and light'un my ceegar."

"Cigar! Hey, that reminds me...want a smoke?"

"Yah, I'll take a smoke. Where you gonna get it? Swim down to New Orleans and get one? Go ahead. I'll be right here. But if you take over three days, I'm go'un home."

"OK you just sit there. I'll be back in two days."

"Where you go'un?"

"On and on. You just sit there."

Twenty Minutes Later

"What's that you got?"

"Grapevine. I cut it off a that stuff over there where we was swing'un."

"Yeah, well where's the smoke?"

"This is it. Grapevine – dried. Gotta get a dry piece. Here, go ahead, stick it in the fire. When it gets burn'un, puff on it."

"Yee – ouch."

"Get it out the fire dummy! Smoke it like them seegars you said you smoked in Jamaica."

"Hum, it works. How'd you know 'bout that?"

"Aw, an old Indian out in Arizona told me. Same one told you about smoke'un in Jamaica."

"That so. That so. Well it's not bad."

"Hey, look at that tow go'un down."

"Yeah, he's move'un."

***

"Hey, big man, I'm hungry."

"Me too. Did you turn the corn again."

"Sure, sure. How we go'un a eat this stuff - with or fingers?"

"You did bring some spoons and forks and stuff, didn't cha? Tell you what. I'm go'na eat mine anyway I can. I guess you can do the same. The bean can's gotta cool, 'cause you gotta kinda drink the beans out. If you want a drink a water, there's the river. Take all you want."

"Oh, yeah, thanks a lot. . . hey, this fish ain't all that bad."

***

"Sit'un here on a stink'un sand bar eat'un fish by the ole Mississippi river – and I'm full. Hey let's have another smoke. I'll go with you."

"No need I brought plenty. Have one."

"I can't believe this. I tell ya I didn't know this would be this way. It's OK. I see what you was talk'un 'bout now. I admit it. I didn't really believe it before. Ya know?"

"A - huh. You know I sometimes think I'd like to just shut

25

down time right here. I look at myself and I think I'm big enough to take care of myself and do whatever I want to do. Still I ain't tied down to no regular work, nor nothing. I think it would be good just to stay this way."

"Might be good a - right, but I don't know how you go'un a do that. Oh - hey - look - here comes another big tow. Look at the lights on that sucker. He's sure moving on with that thing, going down river and all. I'd sure hate to be in his way."

"A -Yeah, me too. A - I do think about this sometimes, even when I'm not out here. I think, 'what's this world all about anyway. Here we are going to school all the time so we can get out and work all the time so we can eat so we can work some more. Is that what this world's all about'?"

"Don't ask me, man. I just do the best I can and don't ask no questions."

"I know, but don't you ever wonder what it's really all about?"

"What's what all about? Suck'un on that grapevine go'un to your head?"

"Maybe, but I don't think so. Look at them stars out there. I read in a book that they's a million light years away."

"They what? What's a bright year?"

"A million light years - *light* years, dummy, you know, how far light goes in a year."

"Oh bull, light don't go no where, Drew. If they're so far away - how come we can see 'em?"

"That's what I don't know. People look through telescopes and stuff and study 'em. And they say they're out there that far."

"Well, let them worry 'bout it. They probably get paid to do that. I don't get paid so I don't worry about it."

"I know, but don't you ever wonder 'bout things like that?"

"No."

"Well, I guess I'm close enough to Missouri. I got that 'show me' way of think'un. Ya know?"

"What did that ever do for you?"

"Noth'un I guess, really. Just can't hep think'un and wonder'un what it's all about?"

"Drew, you nuts. Hey, we go'un a sleep right here by the fire?

"Well, no. The fire'll go out and this ole sand is cold and too hard. See right over there – that row of willows? Well right behind that is a nice dry sandy spot. The willows kinda break the wind and that sand there is deep and soft. Stays kinda warm from the sun. When you lay down in it and kinda wiggle around you sort fit down in it. You ready for that?"

"I guess."

***

"This better?"

"Yeah – is kinda – well it ain't exactly soft, but it's better than that over there."

"Even the stars look brighter."

"Aw, Drew. You go'un with that stars junk again?"

"OK, I was just enjoy'un look'un at 'em."

"You want to look at somethun. Look at them big ole Cottonwoods. Man, it'd be tough to even throw a rock as high as them."

"Yeah, I've looked at 'em before. You know what I can't figure.

"Aw, no what?"

"Well, look at 'em. Like you was say'un. They're big! The wood really ain't good for much, but still it's solid. I mean you get hit on the head with a limb from one and you'd know it. 'En, well big and heavy and solid like they are – and there's hundreds of them – looks like there'd be an awful big hole under ground where all that stuff came from...."

"Drew, you crazy. I tell you where they come from. The seeds fall to the ground and with all the water around here, it waters the seeds and they just grow. That's all."

27

"I know all that. But I still don't understand how a little bitty seed and water can make so many great big trees like that. Where's all the stuff that makes that wood come from? 'An like them stars and all - you know 'bout how for that is....?"

"No, Drew I sure don't! What you care 'bout all that mess anyway?"

"Wait a minute Bo. Think about it...."

"I've done all the think'un 'bout it I'm gonna."

"I know, I guess it don't change anything. But you remember when we was in ole Mr. Lincoln's class and he was tell'un us about how somethun has to get into our eye, like a little bit of energy or somethun, he said, so you know your see'un somethun?"

"Naw, I don't."

"Well, anyway, that's what he said. And that's weird that something from the stars, as far away as they are, get into my eye, 'an yours 'an everybody's, from that kinda far off distance, a light year. 'En light goes a hundred and sum'then thousand miles a second! A second man, think how far that is."

"You think."

"Well, they say the world's about twenty five thousand or sumpthun miles 'round it's middle. I figured it out at home...."

"You figured it out at home! You hard up for somethun to do?"

"Wait a minute. I don't mean I figured out how far it is around the world. I figured about how many times the light would go around the world in a second. I think it would go 'bout seven times around the world in a second! That's move'un."

"You still hard up for somethun to do."

"Maybe, but I penciled it all out. If light goes one hundred eighty somethun thousand miles in a second, then it goes over eleven million miles a minute. And if you times that by sixty to get how far it goes in a hour, it goes over six hundred million...."

"You nuts, Drew."

"Wait a minute, now. If you times that by twenty-four to find out how far it goes in a day, its gets into so many numbers I didn't know what to call them. And then to find out how far it goes in a year, if you times it by three hundred and sixty-five ---- "

"That's it! That's all! You times it by what ever you want. I've heard enough!"

"OK OK, but ain't that some kinda weird?"

"So weird I don't give a hoot. Go dream about 'em. I tell you what Drew, you sure got some kinda worries. When you figure all that stuff out, you go on down and sell it to somebody and give me some of the money. OK?"

"OK. You go on and go to sleep and dream about all them women in Hawaii you know."

"Jamaica."

"Yeah, Jamaica."

***

Next morning the dawn wakes Drew and Bo. Not much left for a breakfast. Little corn left. That's about it. So they take a little swim to wake up and decide to head on back. Swimming back is easier. You can sort of use the current to get you there, if you do it right.

"Drew, you gonna get some corn to take home?"

"Yeah, but lets go down to the other end. I want to get a little more this time. Don't have to swim with it."

"Spose that ole man and his shotgun are out."

"Naw, too early for him. He can't hit noth'un with that thing anyway."

"Maybe, but I don't want him get t'un off no lucky shots."

"OK, here we go. Hey, it's better down here. Must get the early sun on this end."

"I though the sun shined on both ends."

"Aw! aw! Here comes somebody. White pecks. Three of

29

them. One of 'em's big!"

"Ignore 'em."

"They come'un right this way."

Three good ole boys in bibs. An' they aren't going to get off the path for two blacks.

"What you all do'un down here. Steal'un corn?"

"I don't think it's your corn to worry about."

"Oh yeah, well maybe we'll give you somethun to worry about."

The biggest one, quite a bit bigger than Andrew, starts coming right at him. Andrew knew he was in for trouble. He'd faced this before. So, he decided he'd better be ready and he always thought, 'if you have to fight you better get the first punch in, before he's ready and get it in good'.

Andrew watched the big guy. He wasn't paying close attention. His eyes were not on Andrew or his hands. He was glancing from one place to another. Andrew decided next time his eyes moved away from him, he'd let him have it.

One more step and he was close enough. Andrew shot out his left hand towards the big guy's face. It made him blink. That's what Andrew waited for. At that moment he let him have it with his right hand as hard as he possibly could. Pushing with his foot behind him to give him more power. The punch hit him right on the end of the nose. Andrew knew from some little previous experiences that this was a painful place to be hit. Brings tears to your eyes, makes you more than a little sick at your stomach and hurts like crazy.

The big guy went down bleeding and crying. The other two just stood there. Andrew and Bo took off.

"Hey, get outta here!"

"I'm go'un. I'm go'un."

"Cut down here to the tracks and behind those boxcars and we can go all the way down, cut over again and we're home."

"I'm go'un. I'm go'un."

And they did, all the way home.

Well, that's the way it was, an average day. Bo and Andrew had a lot of 'em over the years, swimming, swinging, smoking and laying in the sand wondering. . .what it's all about.
Angels

"Our friend Andrew seems a normal human person. It's good he has a questioning mind. He has opened himself to receive more knowledge. It's one of the first ways that leads to a full understanding. He's young and in one way he is vulnerable to embracing the wrong messages, as is everyone there."

"That is why we must be with him. Questioning as he does, he will not be content to find his true destiny in trivial matters. The direction he chooses to fulfill his life will be critical."

"We will stay with him. Nothing serious has occurred so far."

"True."

Chapter 2
1940

Things were tough - all over. Work was scarce. Andrew was thinking of quitting school and trying to find work. His mother was having trouble putting food on the table. No more good times like in the past. This makes Andrew wonder even more. Why do things have to be this way? Why can't we go on the way it used to be?

***

"Hi Drew. You going over to that white folks' gymnasium tonight?"

"What for?"

"Aw, you know, it's the thing Roosevelt or somebody started. Kids can go to the gym and do sports and stuff. Because it's a government thing, they have a night for us in the white folk's gym. Also 'pose to give the guys who are do'un it a job and all that."

"What's that got to do with me?"

"Well, you can play basketball and – hey, I don't know. Listen, it's free. That's all you got to know. You ain't got nothing to do anyway."

***

"Good thing this gym's where it's at. I don't think white folks would like us traipse'un through their neighborhood."

"Guess not. What we go'na do in there?"

"Tell ya in couple hours."

"Yeah."

"Well, what do you think, Drew? I didn't see you for a while. What'd ya do?"

"Oh, some guy in the back was talking about boxing and – a – I kinda got interested. He said there was an ex-professional boxer coming next Thursday night and several Thursday nights. I guess, to teach guys to fight."

"Gee, I thought you got a good lesson in that the other day at school."

"Boxing's different than fight'un."

"What? You put on boxing gloves?"

"Anyway I think I'm com'un down to see what they go'un to do."

"OK. Well, tell me about it when you get back, cause I ain't go'un."

"OK."

Thursday Night

"Fellows - this is Mr. Hooper. He's an ex-light-heavyweight professional boxer. Now retired.

"He will be your instructor. Mr. Hooper's time is limited, so pay attention. Do what he tells you to do and no fool'un round. Mr. Hooper."

"Hi, men. Mr. Williams is right. We have to get right to it. With me here is one of the trainers from Upstate Athletics Club. I'm going to spend some time showing you some basic things to be aware of when you box. Then you will go in the ring and he will take you through it. Just listen, pay attention and do what we tell you. Now line up over there!"

After the First Session

"Aw, Drew, you get in another fight. What's the matter with your eye?"

"Noth'un. I just learned a lesson from that guy in there."

34

"Oh yeah. That boxing guy? What happened?"

"Well, they put us in the ring right away, with this guy who's a trainer. They were showing us how to step back and cover. I guess I wasn't do'un it right an' he kept telling me if I didn't cover I'd catch one right in the face. I laughed and he showed me, right in the eye. I learned my lesson."

"You did that a' right. I guess you won't be go'un there anymore."

"I don't know. I learned a few things and, like you said, I ain't do'un nothun anyway. And it's free."

"Yeah, ever poke in the snoot I ever got was free, but no thanks. Don't you get into enough hassles at school and all?"

"This different."

"Uh - huh - looks like it."

Weeks Later

"Drew you been go'un to that boxing thing quite a time now. What you see'un in there?"

"I don't know Bo. I kinda like it. Not make'un the mistakes I was. 'Member that first night and I came home with an eye? Well I know if you put your fist in front of your face and some guy hits it, it hits your face almost as bad as when he hits you with his fist. Gotta make a bridge. Take the blows on your fore arms."

"Take you all this time to learn that?"

"Oh no, I just thought you knew what I was talking about because you saw my eye an' all."

"What else you been spend'un your free time do'un?"

"Well, lots a things. We been working in the ring a lot. Ole 'Roper' Hooper don't fool around. He gave us a sheet of paper with all kinds of workouts on it. He said we don't need no supervision for that. But we better do it if we want to get in shape."

"'Roper' Hooper?"

"Funny isn't it? Better not tell him it's funny. They say he used to have a way of coming off the ropes when the other boxer thought he had him and catching 'em by surprise. That's why they call him 'Roper'."

"OK. Tell me what's all this got to do with you? You go'un a win all your fights at school now."

"Maybe. Nah, that's not it really. Just one of those things, you know. Just makes me feel good to be able to handle myself."

"Anything in it?"

"Several guys asked that. Ole 'Roper' Hooper says, 'Don't get any big ideas – but it does happen.'"

"Oh, you think you go'un to make a buck?"

"That's a long way out, Bo, if ever. And that's a big, big 'if'. First I don't know if I want to. Second I doubt if I could."

"He give you any come on?"

"Well, I got a realize this is one of them light years away things - from climbing into a ring for money. But last Thursday ole Hooper chose the ones he said had some small sign of talent. I got chose. He didn't choose many."

"Well, I guess that's somethun."

"I think I earned it. The last thing he did was put us in the ring with that professional trainer and boxer! He wailed the tar out of all of us. I mean when he hits you, the world stops for a second."

"You a glutton for punishment, Drew."

"Yeah, maybe. Ole Hooper say he know we were taking a beat'un, but he wanted to see what we were made of. Blood, I think! Anyway, after it was over – some didn't last – he told me that I had fight'un guts. Then he told me to step over there with the other two he'd picked. That made three of us out twenty-seven!"

"That guy fought twenty seven of you?"

"No, only the ones Hooper picked – eight."

"What comes next?"

"Hooper says we will get some amateur fights, no money, if we want to continue. First around here and then whatever he can arrange. We'll be with some club."

"Um-um. I never thought I'd see you mess'un into somethun like that."

"Well, Bo, tell you the truth, I never did either. But, you know I been think'un....."

"Aw, aw, there you go with your think'un again. I think you better think about what's in this for you. For sure!"

"Yeah, I have thought about what's in it for me. I've thought about what I want to do with me, period. What chance has a black kid like me got. White folks have'un a tough time make'un a living whether they gone to school or not. What you think the chances of me get'un a real good pay'un job...?"

"Well, I think the chances of you make'un any money fight'un is 'bout the same – real slim!"

"Aw, I guess. Well, just forget it. Oh hey, look yonder. The church folks is have'un another do'uns. 'Spose they're go'na do all that sing'un and stuff they did the other night."

"That's choir practice, Drew. My mama goes sometime. You ever watch 'em up close?"

"No, I ain't never been in a church."

"Oh you heathen booger, you. You don't have to go in. See those trees there? C'mon, we just can climb up there and look in the windows. In the summer they always pull 'em down from the top. From up there you can see right in."

"I don't know. Is it that good?"

"Yea, yea, they really get move'un. C'mon."

"Holy smokes, there's a bunch of 'em."

"Oh yea, when poor people get down, they go to the church and start pray'un and sing'un a lot."

"That so?"

"Yeah,"

"Hum. Must be somethun to it. Sure is a lot a people in there."

37

"There's somethun for you to think about, Drew. 'Course there ain't no money in that either. In fact you supposed to give your money to the church. They don't give you any."

"Must be some good reason for people to do that."

"Well, I understand that's a long story. You'll have to get somebody else to tell you 'bout that."

"Maybe I will someday."

Angels

"He needs some help!"

"I know. I know."

***

While Drew was spend'un some of his "free" time learning about boxing, he was also spend'un some of it with an old man he knew in the neighborhood called Uncle Ben and hanging 'round the river like lots of us did.

The old Mississippi is a part of a lot of people's lives in one way or another and Andrew and his friend Uncle Ben were no exception. Ben wasn't Andrew's real uncle. He wasn't uncle to lots of people who called him uncle. In fact most of us didn't know who he was really uncle to and who he wasn't. He was just one of the old characters who had been around as long as anybody could remember. Lived by himself, but was friendly to just about everybody. Seemed like he'd been everywhere and done everything, seemed like anyway.

Well, Andrew, who lived right down there by the river, was especially friendly to "Ole Ben." At first he just stopped and talked to him when Ben was sit'un outside under that old tree by his house. Ben always had plenty of time to talk and seemed to have a way of presenting his opinions on just about anything in a way that was interesting to young people. That especially applied to Andrew, who had a questioning mind anyway.

Andrew first became really close to Ben when they decided

to go to a ball game down in old Cotter Field one time. The black teams could play there on off days, which was most of the time, and didn't have to pay anything. They didn't have any money anyway and ole man Groger who owned it said they kept it cleaner than the white folks did. Maybe that was their way of pay'un for it. I don't know.

Anyway Ben and Andrew went to the ball park together and talked all the way down there, all during the game and all the way back. Then they sat under the tree and talked some more. Seemed like no matter what they got into, Ben always had some interesting way of looking at it that Andrew had never considered before. They walked a certain way to the ball park that Ben explained was to keep the sun out of their eyes while they were walk'un, keeping behind an old factory and some trees did help.

Ben had something to say about most everything that took place in the game. He told Andrew to watch one batter who struck out twice. He said when he got ready to hit the ball, he made too many decisions. Andrew asked him what he meant and when he came up the third time Ben told him to watch his bat. He said he hesitated, drew it back just slightly and then swung. Ben said the ball went by him while he was trying to decide to hit it.

"Gotta only make one decision," Ben said, "that's not to hit it. If you're trying to decide should I hit or should I not, you're take'un too long. Ball's gone by. You step up to that plate ready and prepared to hit every pitch and you start into it. Then all you got to do is decide to stop your swing if it ain't what you want. Sometimes when you've already started a swing. Gotta watch that. But you gotta be there when the ball is and into your natural swing."

He pointed out one other batter that seemed to do that. He got two hits.

Andrew came to see ole Ben more and more after that ball game. Went to a couple others. Ben picked the winner both times. I think he knew something beforehand. One day Ben asked Andrew if he liked to go fishing. Andrew said he sure did and so the very next day they started out. Andrew came by Ben's house with his dad's cane pole and all the fish'un stuff he had in a coffee can. Prepared this time. Ben started out with nothing in his hand. Didn't have a cane pole like most fishermen.

"Where's your pole?"

"Oh, I travel light, Drew. That's women's way of fish'un." Was true. Lots of black women sat down by the riverbank with cane poles trying to catch their supper – all day. Really Andrew knew. He'd traveled light a few times himself.

Anyway, he asked, "How you go'na fish?"

"I got my hook, sinker and line in my pocket along with my knife."

Ben always carried a very large knife. Used it for lots of things.

"There's so many poles down there, I don't see any need to be tote'un 'em back and forth to the river all the time. Just cut one of them Willers and whop the branches off it and you got one. Nice and limber too. Worms is down there. We'll dig 'em."

That wasn't exactly new to Andrew either, but off they went, down to the river. They did live close to the river by town standards, but it was still quite a walk. Ben went pretty slow.

After they left the road and went over the levee, it got kinda thick with Willows and muddy sometimes, depending on how high the river was mostly. Course rain didn't help any either. Soon they came to a long oval stretch that they had to cross - at a narrow place. It was full of old black gumbo mud that kinda melted into black water on top. Andrew and some of the other kids had had a sliding good time on another similar hole elsewhere. Ben wasn't interested in sliding or getting all muddy, which was inevitable, so they walked around to find the narrowest spot. In one place, where it had dried up some, there were funny looking little chimneys all over. They were made of mud – two, three inches wide and three – four inches high.

"What the heck's that?"

"Andrew, ain't you ever seen craw-dad holes before?"

"Yeah, in the ground, but what's that?"

"They's craw-dad holes, only the river gone down and the craw-dads have to dig down to the water. Then they bring up the mud they dug up and pile it in them little chimney circles like that. Watch 'em a minute and you'll see one put some more dirt on top."

Sure enough, pretty soon Drew saw a claw come up and deposit a little clump of dirt in the round chimney built over the hole. Then he'd go down and get another glob.

"Good time to catch craw-dads."

"Catch 'em? How you go'un to catch 'em?"

"Easy. Just get you an ole stick, just long enough to reach the ground and when one of 'em comes up with a clod of dirt and you see that claw, just knock that mud chimney over with your stick and you got you a craw-dad. Go 'head, try it."

"A – just a minute. . . "

"Here I'll cut you one. This one's long enough."

"Now I don't see any."

"Just wait. There, there, there's one. Knock it over. Ha, you got you a craw-dad."

"He's upside down."

"Just roll him over with your stick. Then pick him up by his back. Don't get up too far front, he'll try to pinch you, but he can't if you just keep back from them claws."

"What I do with him?"

"Well some folks say they eat 'em, but they ain't much to 'em and I don't think they worth the trouble."

"What I do with him then?"

"What ever you want. Kids play with them. Pull the claws

off, sometimes. Kids are mean, ya know. Sometimes they see if they can really pinch with them claws. If it's a big'un, they *can* draw blood. Just toss him back."

"OK. Say, we gotta get past this mud hole and it's a long walk around. You gonna wade across?"

"Sure, only don't take you shoes off. No tell'un what's in that old sink hole. I've seen broken glass - sometimes. We can wash 'em off when we get to the river."

Ben's shoes were a real self-custom job. He got them from someone who had thrown them away and obviously were a bit smaller size. But Ben had cut three or so holes right where the little toe was, and in some other places, and made it so he could squeeze in. He said they were made specially for summer wear. (He wore the same kind in the winter.)

Andrew's shoes weren't "air conditioned" but they weren't exactly new either, so it didn't matter. Ben lead Andrew down to a bunch of old logs by the side of a kinda backwater area along the bank of the Mississippi. If you walked out on the logs you could get pretty far out over the river and over a fish hole, according to Ben.

Ben had cut himself a "pole" and picked up some grubby look'un things from under a limb he kicked over and dug a handful of worms with his knife. Ben tested for bottom. If the line went slack or the cork float stayed put, he knew the sinker was on the bottom. If it sorta went with the current if he let it, he knew it was off the bottom. Well, they fished a while. Ben caught one. Drew was just sitting, watching the river. Day dreaming.

Finally he said, "Ben you ever go to that church downtown on Walnut?"

"Oh yeah I go might near every Sunday."

"Hum, Bo and I was watch'un 'em the other night. I can't figure why so many people get so worked up in there. What's so important? Bo says they even pay money to go."

"Well, Andrew I been going a long time and they's still lots

I don't know. But, I kinda dwell on what I do know. Church folks say it's all about love. God loves us and we should love each other. Then there's this Golden Rule. It says 'Do unto others like you want them to do to you'. I started by thinking on just those things and I decided if that's what it's about, I guess that's bound to do a lot of good around here. The rest kinda comes slow and is harder to understand. But it's easier to get to it if you just allow the first things first. The others will come. Sometimes, like they say in Texas, 'It's like slow poison, but it works."

"Yes sir, I guess that's true. I hear people say you got to be saved."

"The Good Lord does that. They say He does that if you accept Him. That's on the inside – what's really you. I think if you love one another and act so, it shows you accept Him on the inside. That's what counts. He does the sav'un."

"Hum, sounds simple when you say it. It seems different when I hear all those folks singing and pray'un an' all."

"Well, Andrew, the way they feel and the way they go about it is up to them. I'm sure they's a lot that just do it for show. But there's another bunch that's just happy and they just naturally get excited about it. Some just keep it to themselves. We all different."

"Aw, man look at them women go'un there. They sure got a bunch a cats."

"Yeah, somebody gonna eat good at their house tonight."

"They must know where the hole is."

"You right. And I been watch'un. Now that they're gone we gonna move on down there. C'mon."

Ben and Andrew ate good that night, too, and many other nights. Andrew liked to fish. He also never forgot the things he learned from Ole Ben during the years of association with him. Some things required a little thought. Others, just trivial things, but sometimes the trivial things led to a little deeper consideration. Like one day Ben and Andrew were sitting under that old tree that Ben used to sit under so often.

And Andrew said, "Mister Ben, what do you suppose craw-dads are good for? You say they really ain't that good eat'un. What good are they?"

"Oh I don't know, Andrew. Lots of things don't seem to be worth anything. Maybe we just don't know what they are good for. Like them doodle-bugs there. . .."

"What doodle-bugs?"

"Oh well, you can't see 'em now. You got to catch 'em first."

"How you do that? Like catch'un craw-dads?"

"Well, not exactly, but sumpthun like that. You got to get 'em outta *their* holes, too."

"What holes?"

"Why, them doodle-bug holes there in the ground. Don't you see 'em all over?"

In the summer, the ground got hard and dry some times. Real hard and real dry. When it was this way, sometimes you could see little holes, a little smaller than a pencil maybe, all over. Doodle-bug holes.

"I see some little holes. But. . ."

"Well, them's doodle-bug holes. Didn't you ever catch doodle-bugs?"

"No, sir."

"Well, great land a Goshen, you never caught craw-dads and you never caught no doodle-bugs. Here let me show ya. Go pull a straw offun that broom over there. OK, now spit in the dust. Now take the broom straw and stir it around in that spit and make a little mud ball on the end of that straw. Don't take much. That's good. Now, just easy now, drop that straw down one them holes. Don't push it. Just let it drop – 'bout half the straw. That's good. Now just watch. When that straw starts to wiggle, pull it up. Don't jerk. Just easy, just pull it right out."

"I'm watch'un."

"Keep watch'un. Usually don't take long. That doodle-bug

don't like that mud on him. He'll start squirm'un around and wiggle'un the straw pretty soon. Then he gets stuck to it 'an you can pull him out. See that? There it is. Pull him out!" "I'll be darn. There is a bug on the end a that straw. That's a doodle-bug?"

"Sure is. Now you know."

"Hum, what's he good for? Can you eat 'em?"

"I don't think so. I don't anyway. Don't know anybody who does. Don't look too tasty."

"No he don't. Too little for fish bait. Wonder what he's good for?"

"Don't really know, Andrew. Lots a things in this world nobody knows what they's for. But does seem like everything is good for sumthun. I always hear folks say, 'They haven't found a cure for that *yet* or they haven't figured that out *yet*.' Like as if they think there's an answer for everything. It's just that nobody's figured it out so far."

"Yeah, I guess."

"I've heard folks say that everything's good for sumthun, even manure. I've heard that even bee stings and snake poison is good for sumthun, but, I don't know what. I guess people just haven't figured this ole world out. Ever time they figure sumthun, they's a whole lot more they find that they don't know. Pra'bly never will."

Angels

"Earth people sure go through some peculiar and long methods to reach some simple conclusions."

"They're earth people."

"Yes, they certainly are."

Next Day

"Andrew! Andrew! I been look'un all over for you. Andrew,

45

your mama's bad sick. There's a whole bunch of people in your house. Better get home quick!"

"Aw, no! - Thank you, Maybell. I'm go'un – I'm go'un."

***

"Oh, here comes her boy. Better let him in here."

"Hello, son. This your mother?"

"Yes sir, it is. What's the matter? Is she all right?"

"Your mother has been...."

"Mama, mama, it's Andrew. Mama what's the matter? Oh, mama".

"Son, I'm sorry to have to tell you this, but I think your mother has left us."

"You mean she's...? Oh no . . . Mama. . . Mama . . . OH – Oh – oh . . . oh."

"We're so sorry Andrew. We tried to find you sooner...."

"Maybe we better just let the boy alone for now. There's nothing anyone can do now. They're com'un for her later."

Andrew stayed with his mother for some time, not saying anything."

"Andrew, would you like to come on over to the house with us for tonight? We're just fix'un supper. They're com'un for your mama soon. You can see her later. Come on now. It'll help you to get a little someth'un to eat and a rest...."

"Thank you Mrs. Bealer. Thank you. If you don't mind, I just want to stay right here for now. Thank you for invit'un me to supper and all... I appreciate it. I just got to be right here for now."

"Well, if that's what you want. You can...."

"Oh Mrs. Bealer, why did this have to happen? My mama didn't do nothing to nobody. And now look. First my daddy and now this. Why? I don't...."

"I don't know 'bout those things Andrew. I guess you just got to trust the good Lord an...."

"That don't seem to help none!"

"I know, sometimes it don't. Especially right now. You just take some time here if you want. We'll be there. You can come over later if you want."

Andrew's grief keeps him awake most of the night. And the dawn of the next day brings the outlook of a very bleak existence. As grief often does, this brings Andrew into a hard realistic look at his position and his future.

Like many Americans and people all over the world, Andrew's life was interrupted by the war.

England - WW II
(Later)

Things went from bad to worse for Andrew. He couldn't get work. He decided to enter the Service – the Army.

Andrew spent several years in the Service going from one place to another within the US. Later he was sent to Europe – England – just outside of London.

Partly because of his stature and partly because he had been very active as a boxer for his company he was assigned to Military Police. These duties gave him the time (or it was arranged) so he could still box in the International Tournament in Europe.

The other experience as an MP opened Andrew's eyes to a side of life he didn't know existed. He couldn't believe the undesirable circumstances and the trouble he witnessed rescuing and often just plain arresting military personnel in their off hours.

Some ended in confinement for a long, long time. *This* certainly wasn't the kind of life he wanted to call his own.

Worrybury Castle

"Hi 'sergeant,' they tell me this is where I'm go'un to bunk."

"Oh sure, 'sergeant', we got two suites open. One over there with a southern exposure and this one. It's closer to the latrine. Take your choice."

"Ha, this one looks comfy. – Andrew Brown – what's yours?"

"My folks call me George Washington Steele. I just go by Steele."

"Hi, they call him that cause he's so hard, hard hearted that is. I'm Roy Crummer. 'Bummer' Crummer, I guess. Welcome to the castle. Just off the boat?"

"Well not exactly. Been in the pool for a few weeks, then they sent me to a Headquarters Co. for a week and then here. You guys been here long?"

"No, no, we came over with Pershing but he went home a while back."

"O-K. Hey, where's the mess hall? Haven't had anything to eat in a while."

"Well you better hit it. It's straight down the end of this street and it closes in about 45 minutes."

"Yeah, they got a special on. All you can eat, same low price."

"Thanks, I'll check it out."

***

"Find the mess hall all right?"

"Oh yeah, had a Spam special."

"Well that's better than the old SOS. Hey, that boxing gear? You here for that big thing the 15th next month?"

"I am scheduled."

"Brown! Sure, I got you here on the sheet. I'm a corner man. I'll be work'un with the guys from the U.S. I'll be in your corner. Used to box myself. Twelve years in the Service. Ended for me when the war started. Haven't had one of these since. I'm too old, anyway. Last time I fought, I fought a German guy. Guess we're still fight'un them in a different way."

"You mean you boxed against the Germans?"

"Sure, before the war. Some of old Adolf's real supermen. They say he actually bred the biggest toughest men with the biggest toughest women. Supposed to be the super race. The pure Aryans - ya know? White guys, blond hair and all. He didn't have much use for us Blacks. Old Jesse showed him a thing back in '36. Remember when he won all them Olympic races?"

"You mean Jesse Owens?"

"That's right. I fought that same year."

"Hum, I knew Hitler was trying to take over Europe and then maybe the world, but I didn't realize he was trying to do it by raising his own breed of people."

"Sure, why you think he's do'un what he's do'un to the Jews. He wants to eliminate them. Then he'll go after the rest of us."

"Hum, I've heard about all the trouble he's been give'un the Jews for a long time. Hard to believe anybody would try to do away with a whole kind of people, like Jews. He'd have to get rid of millions, I guess. That's so bad, it just doesn't seem like that could happen."

"Well, believe it – it is! He'd like to wipe out the English, too, I think, the way he's going about it."

"Speaking of that, you guys ever get hit by any of those V-1 rockets I've heard about?"

"No, not yet anyway, obviously. We're kinda away from the heart of London where most of them hit. Also, they've kinda slowed down. RAF' 's been trying to hit their launchers, I think."

"That's good to hear."

"Didn't they brief you on all this stuff when you were in the pool?"

"No. I'm not sure, 'course, but I think somebody sorta pulled some strings to get me here for the fights. I bypassed some of that stuff."

"Well maybe that's good and maybe it ain't. If you do hear

the 'Banshee' howl, hi-tail it for that door over there across the street with the orange strips – quick! You don't get as much notice for those things as you do for a bomber raid. Ya gotta go!"

"What's the 'Banshee'?"

"That's the siren. You'll know."

"OK."

***

Andrew is given time to train for the up coming fight. He works hard and learns a lot from his new friend, 'Steele'. He is scheduled to fight an English fighter, winner in his last three fights.

***

"Andrew, I'm going to give you a new sparring partner today. He's fought several English fighters and can help you learn their tactics. Now here's some things to think about. All fighters are different, a smart fighter can possibly change his tactics for a fight. English fighters follow more of an established procedure and do a lot of jabbing. They are stand-up fighters and sometimes can be gotten to by coming in and working to the body. When that begins to show a covering up, then you can come in and work to the head. Repeat and watch for counters. OK, that's enough talk for now. Go on and work with Eddie."

Three Weeks Later

"Hey, Roy. Haven't seen you in while."

"Won't for a while, I got that night duty."

"Aw, man, you got my sympathy. Better turn out for the boxing team. I ain't been on it since."

"Well yes, it might work. But I ain't jealous. I wouldn't trade

50

places. Go ahead and box. I'll just keep on chase'un drunks."

WHEE - EE - EE !!

"Great guns. What was that?"

"That's it! That's the 'banshee'! Take off! Hit it for the orange door and fast! I heard it. It's a rocket!"

"I'm right behind you. Go!"

"Gee, guns, can we all get in here?"

"Have to...."

Just then Andrew experiences the loudest noise he's over heard in his life. More than a noise, an impact. Like a great wind hits him all at once. He goes to the floor, blacks out for a second or two. He knows he's recovered, but everything is still dark. The lights are out. His ears hurt and he hears a loud ringing.

"Roy, Roy, you there?"

"I'm here. You OK?"

"I think so. I feel something. Oh, I think my head's bleeding somewhere. Doesn't hurt that bad, but I can feel the blood. You OK?"

"I got something sticking in my side and it must be bleeding, too. Kinda messy."

"Oh, good. lights – little anyway. Man what a mess. Let's get out a here."

***

"Oh no! I can't believe it. Where is everything? Where's the barracks? Andrew, where's George...Steele? He was in the barracks."

"I don't know, Roy. Let's go see what we can find. Watch out, that wall piece is go'un to fall over."

"I can't believe this. I can't see anything that looks like anything. Come on ...."

"The two searched over and over till after dark. Roy had to report for night duty just the same. Andrew continued for hours. Then he went down to the next company's day room and got some sleep. Everything was gone. The barracks was completely destroyed. All their things were gone. They would have to get new issue of everything. But right now, they were more worried about George.

Next Morning

"Hi Roy. Tough night?"
"Night wasn't bad. Some others got it, too. Kinda quiet. I did get some news. Not good. They found four guys in that mess. All dead. One of them was Steele, Andrew. One of them was Steele. I've known him for a long time."
"Are you sure?"
"Yeah, 'fraid so. I saw his dog tags. Didn't see him, but they said there wasn't much to see. I don't feel good. I'm hit'un the sack. Hey, that cut over your eye is still bleed'un. Looks kinda nasty. Better hit sick call. Might need stitch'un up or something."
"Maybe I will. How about you? You OK? Your side?"
"I'm OK, physically."
"Know what you mean. Only known him a few weeks...feel a little pukey, myself. Get some sleep. See ya later."

***

The blood on Andrews's head turned out to be a nasty cut indeed across his right eye. Unfortunately, bad enough that the Army medic would not OK his entry into the big fight he had looked forward to and trained hard for.

This disappointment and the loss of a new but close friend had a sobering effect on Andrew. The reality of the war came home to him, as to many.

Angels

Andrew is in a very explosive situation...."

"Ha ! You've been associated with earth people too long. Are you making, what is their expression, a pun?"

"No, no. I am referring to the realization of the great extent to which the people of earth can go in the wrong direction. And this terrible thing Andrew is becoming aware of, the extermination of so many people."

"You are concerned that this will negatively affect his thinking?"

"Yes, it *is* a terrible thing and others are working with it, I know. I am concerned here about Andrew forming the often accepted opinion that since these bad things happen, there can be no higher power *or* if there is, the higher power would not let these kind of things happen."

"It is a very difficult thing for people of earth level to understand. Too often *everything* to them is contained within the boundaries of their life there."

"Yes, they do not understand that they are, as their "Book" says, 'Created in His image'. Not their physical image obviously, but the real image. Their word is 'soul'."

"Yes, it does of course give them the option of accepting or rejecting anything they choose and there is no limit to how far they will take it."

"One would think they would see that in their own life experience. Their children are born in their image, even physically. They receive love and care but still are free to accept the guidance or not, and to go to any extent in spite of it. It certainly does not prove that the parents are not there, just because the children do unbelievable things."

"Is that what you are afraid Andrew will believe?"

"It is a concern. We must help him through this mental hurdle."

***

Andrew does dwell on many things while in the Service. Being close to life and death brings a new realization to him.

Even though he had heard of it, being closer to the horrors of war definitely makes an impression. For one thing, life can end so suddenly.

Chapter 3
1946

"Bo! Bo! Hey man, long time! How you do'un?"

"Andrew! Dog gone, I thought I'd seen the last of you. You been in the Service all this time?"

"Yeah, after mama died, I didn't have nothing, so I decided to enlist – for three years and the duration. The duration made it a little longer than three years."

"This calls for a celebration. C'mon, I'll buy you a beer."

"OK."

"Say, what's happen'un with you?"

"Oh, I'm com'un up in the world. I was work'un for the cotton seed mill. Now I'm work'un for the soy bean mill. More money."

"You in the Service?"

"Yeah, but not any longer than I had to. You know I was just nineteen when I went in, just full of it like everybody else. War was just a big noisy game, until my first buddy got killed. An then sometimes it was a matter of surviving. Not funny. Folks say 'war is hell,' well that's true, but it sure don't fill it all out. Duration and that was it for me!"

"Don't blame you. With me, well, I couldn't make it on my own. Couldn't get a job. I found out that little ole house we lived in wasn't paid for and I couldn't do it. So, the Service didn't look too bad. At least I ate good."

"Yeah, no bean cans and cat, huh?"

"Aw hey, that was pretty hard to beat."

"Yeah, I'll say. Hey, you ever do any lay'un in the sand and look'un at the stars while you was work'un for your 'rich uncle'?"

"No, didn't have anytime for that. But I did meet some strange guys from different parts of the world. They sure had some different ideas 'bout things. But I kept pretty busy."

"OK. A, what are you go'un to do now?"

"Well, Bo, believe it or not - remember those boxing lessons I took once? Well, turned out I did quite a bit of it in the Service. Represented the Company over here, and when we went to Europe, I fought in several International matches. Actually I did pretty good. Learned to keep my eye covered. Anyway a guy in Chicago has offered to get me in one of the gyms there and opt for some matches."

"So, you really going to go after a boxing career, huh?"

"Well, I gotta do something and I been thinking...."

"Aw, oh, there you go. Still thinking, huh. What did you figure out?"

"Well, you know we can get some of that GI school money and I'm going to look into schools in Chicago."

"What are you going to study?"

"Don't know. They say you can take 'General Studies' until you decide on something."

"Well, seriously, Drew, I think you smart. Nell and I...oh, by the way I got married...."

"You're kidd'un! Well, congratulations! Anybody I know – Nell?"

"Yeah, you know her. Nell was Nell Meadows. She was two years behind us."

"Oh sure, yeah. I sure do. Gosh, she seems so young as I remember her. Guess we all have grown up."

"Well, she's old enough to be a mama come September."

"Bo! You ole son-of-a-gun. Going to be a Daddy! Man, I guess we are growing up! Congratulations again. You a gett'un a little ahead a me here."

"Just do'un what comes naturally, you know."

"Yeah, well good luck to you...and your family-to-be. Say, I'd really like to meet them. Why don't you invite me to dinner

or sumthun? I'll bring my own tator.
"Ha! Done. Finish your beer."

***

"A, Nell! I'm home. Somebody I want you to meet. A – I guess I gotta get serious for a minute. Nell, see this man here? Well if it wasn't for him I wouldn't be here. I guess you wouldn't be *here* either and neither would our baby. 'Member me talk'un about Andrew Brown, my best buddy? Well he pulled me out of the river one time. And now he's back. He's here. Drew, meet my wife, Nell."
"Oh, hello, Andrew. Pleased to meet you. I remember you. You were that other big handsome guy in the 11th grade when I was a freshman."
"Pleased to meet you too, Nell. Thank you, and say, who was the first one?"
"Ha! Three guesses."

***

Drew, Bo and Nell enjoy a very pleasant evening on into the late hours, talking and remembering the good times they had together some years ago...before the War, before the depression, before a lot of things. Those were the good old days.

Next Day

Aw, man I sure hated to say good-bye to Bo and Nell. The Army kinda took me away from all that. Sure brought it back last night. Things were tough, but the personal experiences are just beyond put'un a dollar on. I hate to leave.

Well here's my train. Got a long ride ahead a me....But what really worries me is what an I going to do when I get there. Bo said he thought he could get me on down at the soy bean mill. But, I don't know, it just isn't for me I guess. Huh! What is?"

Drew stood at the back of the train watching the rails go by and seeing the life he knew before slowly fade in the distance. He experienced a kind of sick at your stomach loneliness that he hadn't felt since his mother died.

Chicago

Well, sure ain't nobody here to meet me I'm sure. Can't afford any cab fare. Gotta find these Avery Black apartments. Old Max (the boxing trainer) said he'd fixed it so I could get a room. Cost me twenty bucks extra. I hear apartments aren't that easy to get – after the war and all

***

Well, - "Avery Black" apartments. Some place. Six stories high...

"Wha! Oh, no! You – why don't you watch where your going? Oh, my eggs and the milk...."

"Oh, man! A, hey, I'm sorry. I didn't see you...."

"Well, you should watch where you are going. Now look at that! I've lost my eggs and look at that milk!"

"Miss, I am sorry...."

"Oh sure, so am I...YOU"

"Look I know say'un your sorry don't fix it. Here let me help you pick up this mess ...."

"Never mind. Just watch where you going next time."

"Yes, I will. I know 'sorry' doesn't fix any thing."

"Yeah. You said that. "

"Look, I'm going in the store there and replace the eggs and milk - just as soon as I can get this cleaned up."

"Never mind. I can do it myself...."

"I know, but just a minute. I'm on my way to get the eggs and milk. Let me see what kind it is. Please don't go away. I'll be right back."

"Oh, sure!"

"Good, you're still here. I got the eggs and milk. Please accept them with my apologies."

"Well, that is decent of you. I never knew anybody in Chicago to do that before. Thank you. I'm sorry. I couldn't help being mad. I know these things just happen. You look like your looking for something."

"I guess I just found it. I have an apartment here."

"Oh you do? You must know someone. I had to buy my way in."

"You live here?"

"Yes, I do. A, well I better be going now. Thank you for the eggs and milk."

"Your welcome...a..."

Well, I guess people don't want to be too friendly in Chicago.

At the Gym
(Next Day)

"A, hi! A... I'm supposed to work out here."

"That so? Did ya check at the office?"

"Over there? It's closed."

"Well, beat it. Ya gotta check in first."

"I was told to see Max...."

"Max who?"

"I don't know his last name...."

"Check in at the office, OK?"

"Max told me to just ask for him."

"Aw – MAX! You expect'un anybody?"

"No. A...oh, hey – yeah. Yeah I did tell a kid to come. Brown... you Brown?"

"Yes sir. I am."

"You ain't in the Army anymore, kid - drop the 'sir.' Take a couple laps around the gym and then go on down to the office. I got to get you signed in."

"Yes s...A – a right, I'm go'un."

"Kid fought in the Service. Kinda rough, but he's got some promise, maybe. Sign him up, get his money and send him back here. OK?"

Avery Black - 6th Floor

Man I thought maybe the first day would be easy, a break-in or something. I don't know if I'm broke-in, but I feel like I broke something. Sure am hungry. Hey, elevator's working. First time I've seen it run'un. Oh it's a "run it your self." Well lets go to "one." Hum, can't be there already.

"A , hi."

"Oh! You, hi. Can you trust this thing?"

"I really don't know. This is the first time I've been on it. I guess you won't have to risk your milk and eggs, anyway."

"Ha, no. Well, I've never been on it before either. But I heard it's been down for a couple weeks and never did work too well. You going all the way down?"

"I guess so."

"Well, give it a try. Punch 'one'."

"Well, so for, so good.

WHAM!!

"Oh no. I shouldn't have said anything."

"It stopped. You touch anything?"

"No miss. I just pushed the 'one' button."

"What do we do now?"

"I pushed the 'door open' button, the 'down' button and the 'one' again."

"Nothing's happening. Try the alarm. That's what it's for."

"OK. - Shouldn't you hear it? I don't hear anything."

"Yes, I've heard it before – like a loud bell!"

"Let me see if I can force the door or maybe make enough noise to get someone to help from the outside."

"If we're on the fourth floor, there's not many people there.

They had a fire and most of the rooms near this end are being fixed over."

"Well, I believe it. I can't raise anybody. I can't hear anybody and I can't force this door."

WHAM!!

"Oh no. Oh!!"

"Hold on. Here let me help you...."

"I'm OK".

"We dropped down. Hope this thing doesn't go all the way."

"Me too".

"Gotta find a way outta here."

"There's supposed to be an escape hole in the top. Maybe that's it there."

"Guess I don't know much about elevators...Except for a few I saw in the Service. They didn't have many back home."

"Well I've lived in Chicago a long time. But I still don't know anything about them, either. I do know some of the holes can be pushed open from inside. Want to try?"

"Yeah. I don't know how I'm go'un to reach it. Need something to stand on. There's nothing here. Wait, let me see if I can jump up and push it...No luck."

"I have an idea, if you want to try it. If you can lift me up, maybe I can push it open."

"I – a – well OK."

"It's all right. Just go ahead and pick me up. We have to do something to get out of here. I don't think anybody is ever going to hear us. It's OK, go ahead. Can you lift me?"

"I can lift you, if you're OK. Hang on."

"Its all right. Go ahead – a little more. I think there's some kind of latch. Yeah, now hold me, I'm going to push. It went! It's open! OK, let me down."

"Wow, you did great. Didn't hurt you, did I?"

"No, I'm OK, but I wonder how we're going to get up through that little hole."

"Well, I was just think'un. If I put my foot up on that control thing and give myself a push maybe I could grab hold, now that's it's open, and pull myself up. Then I'll get you up some way."

"Can you do that?"

"Well, like they say, only one way to find out."

"Oh! Oh! Be careful."

"I'll get it. I'll try till I do. – Got it."

Drew manages to pull himself up through the small hole. Then turning around and reaching down he tries to bring her (her name is Amy) up also.

"Wait a minute. I have to figure some way to hold myself while I pull you up. There's something here, seems solid. If I can hook my leg around it and hold, maybe I can pull you up. Can we do that? I don't want to leave you alone in that thing."

"Well I appreciate that. I don't want to be here, either."

"OK grab hold of my hands. Ugh! Hold on!"

"I'm slip'un...."

"Grab me around the neck. Go on - we gotta get out a here some way."

"OK, I am."

"Sorry, but I don't see how to do it any other way."

"It's all right; I understand. I just want to get out of here too! Oh, I'm almost there."

"OK, now just kinda sit on the edge. Let me try to figure out what we got here. Sure is dark in here."

"Really. Be careful."

"Yeah, I will. I think I'm on a level place now. Let me help you stand up, and then step over here. Take my hand."

"Oh yes. This is better. I can stand. What are we going to do? We're still on the elevator."

"I know, I think I'm beginning to get a little used to the dark. I'm almost sure that's a door right there. We're not lined up to it. I think that's why it's stuck. Ouch, I just kicked a piece of wood – 2x4. I'm going to use it to pound on the door, maybe get someone. Stay where you are a minute."

Andrew's pounding this time brings the 'super' and he tells them how to move the lever on their side. And with his help on the other side, they get out.

"Oh, thank you, Mister Simpson. I'm sure glad to be out of there. And thank you for helping me, Mr. – I sorry. I don't even know your name."

"Glad I could help you. I'm Andrew Brown. I'm afraid I don't know your name either."

"Brown - Andrew Brown! You Andrew Brown? You gotta be kid'un me. Well, I'm pleased to meet you, Mister Brown. I'm Amy Brown."

"You must be kid'un *me!* Amy Brown? Well, it certainly is a pleasure to meet you. And I have to say, I feel like I know you already. After all, I have bought you groceries, and – a – well, after that elevator thing and all I feel like – a – I could use a little relaxation. Would you consider having a coffee or something? I never met anybody named Amy Brown before."

"Sure, sounds good. I could use a little relax right now myself. Shurpes?"

"Shurpes? What's Shurpes?"

"Oh that's *the* place around here and it's just around corner...."

"Sounds good to me. Let's go."

***

"I guess there are other Browns in the world but still seems kinda odd meeting someone with the same name. You said you lived in Chicago a long time. You born here?"

"No, actually I was born in a little town south of St. Louis - moved to Chicago later - much later. You said you didn't live in Chicago?

"Gosh, no. I'm not a city boy at all. I was born in a little ole river town called Cairo. All the way to the end of the state."

"I've heard of it. What are you doing in Chicago?"

"Long story. Things were tough at home. Wasn't so bad till my folks died – we had fun at first, but then, with no jobs, I went into the Service – did some boxing and that's what brought me here. I would like to go to school but I don't know what for. I'm not sure if I want to be a fighter, even if I could."

"Interesting."

"Hope so. What do you do here in Chicago?"

"I wanted to be a nurse but couldn't afford the schooling. I did manage to get my LPN license."

"What's that?"

"Licensed Practical Nurse, next best thing, I guess."

"Sounds good to me. Say, I have to say one thing. You sure handled your self well in there, in that elevator. Some people would have panicked."

"I suppose so. I think it's because I've learned to look at things in a little different way than some. Even different than I used to myself. Hard to explain...."

"Maybe I understand a little about what your say'un. I think about things a lot and I have changed my ideas and the way I think quite a lot in the last few years. Kinda strange...."

"Oh hello, Mr. Simpson."

"Don't mean to but in. S'cuse me. Just wanted to be sure you two didn't get hurt or anything in there did you? You're OK?"

"No, no, I mean, sure we're fine. A, well I guess I should speak for myself. I'm OK...."

"I'm fine. Just inconvenience mostly, with me anyway. Yes, I'm fine. But thanks for checking anyway."

"Well, I just wanted to be sure. Sorry I bothered you. See ya later then."

"OK, see ya later."

***

"Amy – a, I haven't had anything since lunch. Seems like a long time ago...."

"I sorry. Didn't mean to keep you...."

"You're not keeping me from anything. I enjoy your company. Just thought you might want something also."

"I guess lunch has been a long time ago for me, too, and the elevator thing and all. Sounds good."

Amy and Andrew have dinner and some long conversation while getting better and better aquatinted all the time.

***

"Oh, can you believe it's 10:40. Maybe I better go. Six o'clock is going to seem gruesome in the morning and I still have some things to do."

"Me, too. Say I really enjoyed talking to you. I don't think I ever talked to anyone who had some of the same thoughts as I do and was willing to listen to some of mine before. Say, mind if I walk you back? No elevator this time."

"Ha! OK."

Five Flights to Amy's

"Oh, this is almost as bad as the elevator. Well, no, that's not true. At least we can get off the stairway."

"Yeah, right. Say a, Amy would you consider another Shurpes or something, sometime? Have to stay late tomorrow. But, say, Wednesday? 'Bout seven? I'll come by."

"Love to. See you Wednesday then. Bye bye."

"Bye – goodnight."

***

When Andrew went to bed that night he didn't go to sleep for quite a while, although he certainly was tired enough. *I can't get over it. That gal I ran into. She sure is something different. Hard to understand really. Right now, I seem to be excited about talking to her, to say the least. It was so different than any experience I ever had with any other gal.*

I felt like I didn't have to put up any sort of front or I just didn't. I wasn't planning what I wanted to say because I wanted to show off or try to influence anybody or anything. Made me think of what people say sometimes like – 'I feel like I've known her all my life.' She was so easy to talk to and more than that I felt something very personal. Like I wanted to reach out and touch her or something. Not sexy. Not that she wasn't that too. As a matter of fact, real nice. Couldn't help noticing that in the elevator.

Yeah, well that's true and that I can understand. Um, yeah – nice. But this other thing is what gets me. I just felt so easy with her. Talked about stuff I've never even said out loud to anybody, but I felt perfectly natural talk'un to her about it. And I just have this real good excited feeling – real good.

I know one thing. I can't wait till Wednesday. Got a notion to skip out early and go see her tomorrow.

***

Strange, how some of the same type of thoughts are going on in someone else's head just one flight below. Strange, but nice.

Chapter 4
Boxing and Back at the Gym

Some months later – Lots of training and lots of meetings with Amy have gone by. Their relationship becomes stronger and deeper as time passes. And the serious conversations are more frequent.

"Well, Brown, you been hang'un 'round this place long enough. These club fights are OK for training, but I got you scheduled for one the 16th that'll be the first real card you've had. You get fifty bucks if you fight – win or lose."

"OK. Who am I fight'un?"

"Guy called 'Killer Miller.' Stupid name. Don't pay any attention to that. I'll show you how to get to him. You're on the card with a bunch of other guys. You'll fight first. Three rounds."

"OK."

"Go get your workout and then hit the bag. I'll be over after a while. Got you a new ring partner for this one. He's fought Miller. He can help you."

"OK."

17th

"Andrew! What's the matter with your face? Come in here; let me see."

"It's OK, Am. Had that fight last night – you know. I won, Am – I won. The guy wasn't nearly as tough as I thought."

"Oh yeah? What is this? One of those 'you should see the other guy' things?"

"Aw, it's not that bad. I got a cut and my eye's a little puffy."

"A little puffy! Ha! That *is* you under there, isn't it? I'm not sure."

"Well, I guess it was a *little* tough. Max said it was an 'action fight,' for a three rounder."

"Really? That eye. Does it hurt?"

"No. Hey! Max says this gets me a little recognition. I go up a notch. Better fight next time."

"Oh fine! Where do I go to see you, the hospital?"

"Well, sure, if you bring flowers."

"Not funny."

"Oh, worried about me, huh? Well, maybe more good came out of this fight than I thought. I think this needs a little care. Right here. Want to...?"

"You! What if I am? What about that school you talked about? You go'un to chuck that for this boxing thing?"

"Wait a minute, Am. Don't go make'un too much of this. I gotta do sum'thun. These side jobs don't get it. 'Course fifty bucks don't pay a whole lot of rent either. Really I'd like to do something different. Something. I just don't know what right now."

"Well, you said you wanted to go to school. But, you didn't know what to study. Andrew, what really moves you? I remember some of the things you talked about, like not just spending your life working so you can pay your bills...."

"I know. It's strange, really. I do feel like I want to do something. I don't really think it's boxing or stacking boxes either. Then there's the other thing. A guy's gotta eat regular, too. Can't just hang around and shoot pool."

"Maybe it would become more clear to you after you went to school a while. That might help you see what your look'un for."

"Maybe. Seems like a lotta commitment for some'thun I don't even know if I...."

"And maybe you might even seek a little help from The Man upstairs."

"I have thought about that. You keep mentioning it. Don't know a lot about that. Guess I need to think on it some more."

"I know, you've said that. And I know you want to be sure before you accept something. You told me how you liked to check things out and know the reasons for things and so on. It just seems you are in an uncertain position right now and that's what the Big Man is all about. He's there for help in times like these. I don't know why, but I do know there's a lot of confusing things in this world, and when they get to you - well, that's when you get a little help. All you got to do is accept it."

"I wish I knew that was true. It sure would help me if I *knew* that for sure."

"Well, you think about it some more. Remember you're dealing with God stuff. The real proof and knowing comes in a different form, but it's just as real. And better."

"Yeah, I was just think'un back about a time I was fish'un with a friend - Ole Ben. Did a lot of fish'un I guess. He said accept'un God was, in one way, like get'un a cold. 'Course get'un a cold is bad and know'un God is good, but sometimes you just get it. You don't know where it came from or how you got it. But you know for sure it's there. I never thought that was a good example because get'un a cold is bad and your try'un to get rid of it. But I do understand, I think, what he was try'un to say. You can't take it out and hold it in your hand, but it's there just the same."

"Well, since we're talk'un about old friends, it reminds me of a time with one of mine. He was like you. He said he had to know, said if he had some proof it would make a big difference and then he could get into it. Well, he said he thought a long time and finally this convinced him there was a god. He said he threw out everything – what his folks told him and even the Bible. Then he said he just thought about cold facts. He decided that there had to be a god because something had to have been there always. And that something is God. Can't start something from nothing, he used to say. Then his belief grew from there. That's what he said."

"Hum, well that is get'un down to it. I guess you got to start somewhere and if you got a real solid base then you can't shake it and you *can* even build on it."

"That's kinda what he said."

***

Weeks and weeks later – much more time with Amy. Andrew is undefeated!"

Angels

"Andrew is still searching and Amy is helping. He just has to get these earth things behind him. It is the way sometimes."

***

"Oh Am, I'm feeling better. I got a real fight com'un up. Be a while, but I've signed. Am, I'm actually the main event in this one and even more money than the last!"

"Well, I guess that's good."

"Aw, I know your not all that excited about boxing. But this is big. Even got my picture down at the gym on the bulletin board. Max says there's a write up in the paper, not just a schedule of fights like before."

"Um, so you're big time now."

"Well, move'un in that direction. And it feels good! Am, you got to come see this one. Please, I can get you tickets. Bring a friend if you want."

"I don't know Andrew. You know I don't like seeing people beat up on each other...."

"Aw, come on Am. It would help me, know'un your there root'un for me."

"Well, I'll think about it."

"Good, I'm go'un to get the tickets anyway. I don't have to pay noth'un for 'em. They complimentaries."

"Good, I would'un want you to spend money for nothing."

"Aw Am, what can I do? I'm sorry. I don't want to cause you no trouble. It's just that I'm proud of what I've accomplished so far and I want you to see."

"I know, and I can understand you've worked hard to get here. I'll be there and I'll be root'un for you. It just takes a little getting used to. OK?"

Back at the Gym - Fight Instructions
(Later)

"Brown, hey, c'mere. Come on down to the office a minute I got somethun you need to see."

"OK."

"We got some mov'un pictures of this guy you're fight'un in his last bout. I want you to see 'em and study 'em and then put 'em to practice with Raymond here in the ring. Ya hear?"

"Sure. OK."

"A - right. Now watch. His big gun is his right, just at the time you're breaking off, to catch you off guard. Now watch. Here it comes! Watch his right! Just as they part. See it? There it is. Hold it there.

"Now, look where his left is. Down, OK. Now you got to counter him right there. Look at that opening. You could hit him with a base fiddle! But it don't last. You got to get it in there. Now, if you see it come'un, good, be ready. If you don't and he hits you, you got to counter, anyway. When he's close, know where his nose is. Know it so you can throw a punch and hit it whether you can see it or not – hard. Also you got to keep a good base under you, like we showed you. Even when your move'un, don't let yourself get unbalanced. And when you throw that punch, don't telegraph it! Be ready. If you're hit, fire it off. If you have to cover, do it after you counter. Get it in, have it in the right position. You know, you don't draw back and then throw it.

"Now watch it again with Raymond here, and then get in the ring. Raymond's going to give you a real go, but he's been told to give you that opening. You better learn to take advantage of it. OK, go full speed and no pulling punches. He'll be wear'un pads, so go all out. Got it?"

"Yeah, I got it."

"Well, I don't think you have yet, but you better get it!"

Fight Night

"OK, remember what I told you. Don't get into a toe to toe with this guy. He's too big. He'll tire you out, even if you think you are get'un the best of him. You got to counter. Watch your shots. Don't try to win the fight in the first rounds; you're go'un ten, you know. Work on him, pick it up as you go. Don't let him po-boy you. OK? And remember that shot we worked on. Use It! Got it?"

"A - huh – I got it."

"Ya better! Go!"

After the Third Round

" Now you're go'un. OK, you got in there good that time. He's pick'un up his jabs. I think he's try'un to keep you away. That's a change for him. I think you hurt him, but don't let him fake you. If he starts that again, watch his right. Come around to his left and watch for an opening. Your do'un great, now keep it up! Go!"

After Six

"You OK? Good, good! You did just what I told ya. That move worked. You got him good. I think you could have broke his nose. He's bleed'un all over the place. That'll slow him down. He can't breathe. Now get in there again. Keep at it, but

72

watch him. He's an experienced fighter. He'll suck you in. Stay solid and covered! Ya OK? Ya hear? OK, go!"

After Seven

"Great kid, great! You got a knock down! You got him on the ropes, but you gotta finish it. Be careful! He still has a punch. He should be catch'un on and try'un to adjust. Watch for change in his style. Keep the pressure on but don't open yourself! OK?"

***

Round eight becomes bloody. Andrew dominates the fight. At the bell he has pounded his opponent at will. Only the bell saves him.

It becomes readily apparent in round 9 that it is just a matter of 'how long'? Andrew rocks his opponent with solid right hands repeatedly. He staggers. The referee steps in, looks at him. Allows the fight to continue. Andrew sets him up and then drops him hard to the canvas with a right hand that hurt even to watch.

Andrew is jubilant. The crowd roars. He manages a look in Amy's direction. His opponent is still flat on the deck.

On the Way to the Locker Room

"Amy! Amy! Hey, let her through. I did it, baby. I did it! Feels good, doesn't it?"

"I guess so. -You all right?

"Never better! This is it! Hey, give me a hug! This is what I was look'un for. Amy! Amy! Baby – aw – man!"

***

The paper's sport page has a story the next moving. But the headline story is not about Andrew, but his opponent who is still in the hospital and *still* unconscious! His condition is critical and the long term outcome a question.

"Aw, Amy, I never expected anything like this. I don't know. I just thought about winning. They told me I had him go'un and I shouldn't let up. It actually felt good at the time. I could see he was go'un down. It made me feel stronger. I came on harder. It felt good right then."

"You had no way of knowing Andrew. They taught you to do that. I've heard of it happening before...."

"What happened to the guy who did it?"

"I don't know."

***

Andrew doesn't show up for the next two scheduled workouts at the gym.

Max comes to see him.

"I know what's bothering you son, but you gotta go with it. You didn't do anything wrong. It's just the fight game! You were supposed to do what you did. That's what you trained for. That's what the crowd come to see – a real fight. They would have booed you if you stepped back and didn't fight your best – didn't give 'em a real fight. Anyway, it was that ref's fault. He should of stopped the fight if it was that bad. How did you know? He might have been fake'un."

"He wasn't fake'un."

"You know that now, but you didn't know that then. That's why you had to keep go'un. *It's not your fault!*"

"Maybe, but I'm the one that hit him....It's his blood on my gloves."

"I know, I know, son. You'll get over it. I've seen it before. Hey, think about it! You won a big one! Relax. Enjoy it. Go see your girl friend. Take a couple days. But don't take too long. The best thing to help you get over this is to get back into training. Hey, remember – you won. You won a big fight, and I'm proud of you."

Andrew went back to the gym. He worked hard. He did what Max told him, day after day. Also he kept track of his last opponent's progress. It wasn't much. He remained semi-conscious, never showing any real signs of recovery. It ate on Andrew. He tried not to think of it but it showed in his training. He threw punches but not with the great intensity as before. Max sensed it and drove Andrew harder and harder. He scheduled another fight as soon as possible, of course. Each fight was tougher than the one before and this one was no exception.

Andrew talked to Amy of the coming fight. It was for a lot more money. His picture had been in the paper. After all, this was what Andrew wanted and he was being successful at it.

"Well Amy, the big one's tomorrow night."

"I know. Too well."

"You're going to be right down front."

"I know that, too."

"I know that you're thinking of that last fight. It wasn't pretty! Everybody tells me to forget it. That's the fight game. I guess it's happened before. I got to concentrate on this one...."

"Well, I guess you better, so's you don't get yourself hurt. OK?"

"Yeah, I'll be OK."

Fight Night

At first the fight is somewhat a repeat of the last one. Andrew has been trained well. He dominates the fight.

In the sixth round, his opponent tries to alter his style in order to gain a much needed advantage. In doing so, he drops his guard for an instant and Andrew takes advantage and lands one of those damaging rights. It brings blood to his opponent's face immediately.

Max is excited and shouts to Andrew to follow and capitalize on the break. It's as if Andrew can't hear. It's a turning point in the fight. But not for Andrew, for his opponent. The fight becomes a defensive "waltz," as Max says. The real action has definitely left. Some boos are heard at the end. Andrew manages a draw!

At Amy's

"Andrew, you better let me look at that cut again...."
"It's OK. That's not what's bothering me right now. I think I need another hug. Little different kind this time, I think?"
"Um. You hurt somewhere else?"
"Yeah, bad. In my head. Amy, I couldn't do it! I just couldn't do it. As much as I tried to get 'up' for this fight, and Max pushing me, I just couldn't do it."
"You mean fight?"
"Yeah, I mean *fight*. Not like I was supposed to. Not like I should have to win the fight. Not with the desire I had in the first fight. Amy, somewhere late in the fight, 7 – 8th round. I don't know. He started to look like McKibbon, the guy I fought in the last fight. The guy who's still in the hospital! Might as well be dead. When he came towards me with the blood on <u>his</u> face, I saw McKibbon!! Amy! I saw Mckibbon's face! Mckibbon's face, Amy! I couldn't hit him. Not like I did before anyway. Good thing I learned to cover early in this racket. I just rode it out. I don't think I can ever hit anybody like I did. Amy I don't ever want to set my foot in the ring again! I don't know what I want to do."
"You mean that?"
"I sure do! I just couldn't go on.... I don't know what I'm going to do."
Amy holds up her finger.
"Your making some awful big statements here, Mr. Brown. Not long ago you told me this was it! You sure you're sure about what you're saying?"
"Amy, you don't know what I just went through. It pulled

my insides out. I know your wondering if this is just a sudden thing without any deep thought. But it's been in my mind a long time. Believe it or not, this boxing thing never really fit. *Yeah*, I know – what I said and all. But I was so desperate to make something of myself, and I didn't know anything else. I guess I was happy just because I thought I had found my place in this world. Well I still don't know what my place in this world is, but I know it ain't boxing! Never, never again....What *am* I going to do!?"

Amy holds up that finger again looking Andrew in the eye.

"I have an answer for you. I know what you can do...."

"What?"

"Andrew...you can marry me...that's what. Will you?"

"WHA! Am! What did you say. Will *I* marry you!?! Amy! Amy."

Andrew is actually shaking.

"Amy, honey, baby, you know I love you. You – you asked me to marry you. Honey, here I am a washed out fighter and box stacker...."

Amy puts that finger to his lips.

"Andrew Brown, don't talk to me about boxes and boxing. I asked you to marry me. Well?"

I think Andrew is shaking even more, but he manages to kiss Amy like never before.

"Is that a 'yes'?"

"Of course it's a yes. You...Amy, you. But I'm supposed to propose to you. I don't want you to be tied up with a washed out fighter, who's got nothun. That's why I waited. I wanted this to be good and we have a good life, not be poor and have to work hard all...."

The finger again.

"I don't want to hear any more. I want to do whatever we do together. That's what's important."

"Amy, I *do* love you! I...I... Aw, what are you go'un to do, make a grown man cry?"

77

"Go ahead...I love you, anyway."

"Aw, Amy, you know...I never felt so good in all my life. You, *you* asked *me* to marry you! I can't believe it! Wow, what do we do now? Go look at rings or somethun? Well, maybe at least... Shurpes huh?"

Andrew and Amy do end up at Shurpes. A place where they have spent many hours – into the wee hours many times – talking about all the things that two people talk about when they're in love. Even before they realized they were in love. Although it did catch on right from the beginning.

This time there is a mixture of ecstatic happiness, since they both have expressed their love for each other right out loud, and also some serious talk about what to do next, mostly concerning Andrew. They have both talked about school for Andrew and Amy tells him again. She's not only willing to work while he goes to school but she tries to impress upon him that this is the thing she wants. Andrew has been groping for life's answers and a direction for his life for a long time. It seemed to lead him to think it was boxing. But he learned a lesson the hard way. It's not.

Andrew, of course, expresses the feeling of uneasiness, to say the least, thinking of having his new wife working to send him through school. Although he doesn't express it exactly, he has the thoughts running through his mind of his mother – how hard she worked all her life and how little they had. He doesn't want this to happen to Amy. Amy, who always has the best come-backs, tells Andrew that's exactly what she's trying to avoid. Even more than that, she tells Andrew she wants to find the thing in his life and in hers that they both can share and really dedicate themselves to. Amy reminds Andrew that working together towards something they both want brings them even closer together.

They both realize this is the ultimate of fulfillment and happiness in life. Andrew is still a bit, more than a bit, uncertain about just exactly what he wants to do. Andrew agrees to go to school. And he feels good about he and Amy living and working together.

***

They did look at rings and now they have to plan a wedding. Wedding bells were relatively simple for the Browns. They didn't have a lot of friends in Chicago and of course they didn't have a lot of money either. They set a date and decided on the little church not too far away, one they had attended together a few times.

Wedding Day

Andrew goes down to Amy's apartment and gets approval of the suit he's wearing, only one he has.

"Hey, honey babe, you really look sharp. Maybe we ought to get married every day."

"You tell'un me I don't look sharp all the time?"

"Come on, you know better than that. I...."

"Andrew, there's somebody at the door. Wonder who that could be?"

"I don't know, but I don't want any. I'll see - - - BO! NELL! I don't believe this. What you do'un here!?

"We came to the wedding. What else? Nice to see you."

"Well, great guns! Nice to see you too....Hey how did you know? How'd you find us? Hey, wait a minute. Why's everybody laughing? Amy, Bo – hey what's go'un on here? Amy, you in on this? How *did* you find us? I mean...."

"Oh, us women have ways you all don't know about. Right, Amy?"

"Yes, it's called telephone information, but something more important....who's this with you?"

"This is Lori Ann. Named after my grandma. She's six, six months that is."

"Oh, I was named after my grandma, too. She was the

79

daughter of a slave, long time ago. Somewhere back in South Carolina I think. She was an Amy, too. At least that's the story I heard. No one kept any sort of records then. Oh Nell, she's beautiful. You must just love her to death."

"Yeah, she does. I think the expression is, 'spoiling her rotten.'"

"I believe that. Guess I would, too. Hey, you two, I don't know how you did it, but I'm sure glad you did. Amy, I didn't know you knew Nell, how...."

"I didn't. Except for a few conversations on the phone. Nice to meet you in person, Nell - and Bo."

"Really nice to meet you too, Amy. This is great."

***

If you count the importance and the enjoyment of a wedding by the size, Andrew and Amy's wouldn't get many points. But if you count it on emotion and pure enjoyment it was out of sight – for all five. But mostly for Andrew and Amy.

(Ever see the bride and groom cry at a wedding?)

Post Wedding

After all of the excitement of the wedding and honeymoon were over, Andrew and Amy settled down to face their future. Both agreed. it was school for Andrew and they wanted to start as soon as possible.

***

The choice of schools was narrowed down some by the consideration of money and availability. Many veterans were still crowding the schools and also there was the concern of how to get there.

But, there were schools in and near Chicago and a little El and subway ride couldn't be a deterrent if you really want to go. Even if you had to do the same to go to work after school.

Angels

"Andrew is taxing his physical body."

"Yes, many do. It does show he has developed a strong desire to reach the goal he has set for himself. That is good!"

"True. True. It is good and we will continue to support him."

At School

Andrew's inquisitive nature is still with him - even in the classroom. Sometimes it's rewarding, sometimes embarrassing. But rewarding even when it's embarrassing. He has to share it with Amy.

"Hi, babe. Long hard day at the office. How 'bout you?"

"Oh, the same I guess, only I didn't have to go to school first. Have a bad one today?"

"Well, not really I guess. In fact, kinda interesting. I was in that Science class. Somehow the old Prof. got into evolution. And he was going on and on and I must have gotten a silly streak on somehow. It reminded me of an old uncle I used to have. I thought he was a little weird at the time, but later I rethought some of the things he said and they made me think. Doesn't take much, I guess."

"Your uncle, huh? What did he have to say?"

"Lots of things. The one I remember most and I thought the funniest at the time was, 'Which came first the chicken or the egg?' He must have said that a hundred times and then he'd laugh. For some reason after the long spiel by the Professor, I held up my hand and asked him that. I wanted to know where the chicken came from. Everybody laughed."

"I bet."

"He acted a little mad and then said, 'To answer your question I think the chicken evolved from one minute single cell millions of years ago. You have to enlarge your thinking.

It happened over a very long period of time from a very small beginning."

"I said, 'I would have as much trouble understanding where the very small beginning came from as I would the chicken'. They all laughed again except ole Prof. Milligan. He said he thought we'd heard enough about chickens."

Andrew became the most popular member of the class after that, except with Prof. Milligan.

Andrew's time in school was a paradox in a way. Sometimes it seemed long and hard and time seemed to drag. Yet at other times, and when he'd look back on it, it seemed like the time just flew by. You know how that is. You say, 'I can't believe it's two years already!'

Sometimes things in the past seemed like another world. But one day, in the mail, something brought a lot of it back.

"Andrew what's the matter, more bills?"

"Well, yeah that, too, I guess. But Am, I got a letter here that really shakes me up. It's from Bo. An old friend of mine died. A real good old friend, Uncle Ben."

"Aw, I'm sorry Andrew. Where is he, back home?"

"Oh yeah, he was raised there. Maybe did some traveling, but he would never live anywhere else."

"He was your uncle?"

"Not really. Uncle Ben was 'Uncle' to everybody. I knew him since I was little. We spent a lot of time together and did a lot of things. And after my Daddy died he sorta filled in. Ya know?'

"Sure. You go'un to the funeral?"

"Yeah, I sure would like to but I think that's out of the question. We couldn't possibly afford it."

"You want to go don't you?"

"Aw, Am. Don't. You know it's impossible for us. We're hav'un trouble making it now. We can't afford a trip to Cairo."

"Andrew, I've heard you mention Uncle Ben before and I think I know what he meant to you. We can get a ticket on that

IC train. You said it goes right through there. I'm sure Bo and Nell would put us up for one night or two. When's the funeral?"

"Amy baby, I love you when you do things like this and I appreciate it. But, you know we can't do this. Please."

***

Next thing Andrew knows, he's on the Illinois Central train headed for his hometown down south.

Back in Andrew's hometown (a very small town) it seems everybody knows and is affected by the passing of Uncle Ben. The funeral is taking place at the local Baptist Church. Lots of people are at the church already and the funeral is tomorrow. There is a big flower wreath all around the door.

Andrew learns that the funeral will not be in the church at all, but in the large yard area behind the church. A portable makeshift alter is being put up now. Andrew wanders over to see what's happening.

"Why hello Andrew. Andrew Brown. My, haven't seen you in a long time. And would this be Mrs. Brown?"

"Oh, hello, Reverend. A, yes this is my wife, Amy. Amy, meet Rev. Johnson. Rev. Johnson was here when I was growing up."

"Yes, yes. Been a long time. Say, Andrew, I wonder if you would want to do something here to pay respects to our departed brother. I would like to have two or three people give a testimony, that is pay their respects to Uncle Ben here – at the funeral. Just say a few words, ya know? Doesn't have to be long."

"Why yes, I guess I could do that Reverend. Anything in particular you think I should cover?"

"Just speak from the heart, son. Just tell some of the really good things you know about Mister Ben."

"Yes sir. When do I do that?"

"At the funeral. I'll tell you when."

Next day, a large crowd assembled behind the church for the funeral of Uncle Ben. There was much singing and several people spoke. The Pastor seemed to search for some connection to the Bible concerning Ben. Finally it became Andrew's turn.

"I am deeply grateful for this opportunity to speak concerning a departed close and good friend. When Reverend Johnson asked me to say 'a few words,' I asked what I might speak about. 'Just speak from your heart' he said. I thought about that most of the night. There were so many things. Uncle Ben influenced me as I think he did many people in a positive way that always seemed to have a certain special and often personal meaning.

"It would be difficult to relay the impact he had on me at this time. I can't put it into words, even yet. As I look out over this crowd, I see black and white. I see rich and not so rich. Men, women, young and old and I see an awful lot of you. I say, here before me is the testimony to Uncle Ben. No one I have ever known has touched so many people. You – you are the testimony to him; you who have take'un time off from your personal lives to be here to pay your respects to a man who has certainly earned it."

"I thank you and I know if Uncle Ben was looking over my shoulder he would have a smile on his face. A smile I will never forget, on the face of a man I will never forget. Thank you."

The funeral did not come to an end at the church. It only moved, right down the middle of the street, on to the cemetery. Almost everyone followed – on foot. Little groups here and there would just begin singing. Some took the big wreath that was over the door and carried it all the way to the cemetery and then placed it by the open grave. Hours later, people were still bringing flowers and coming by to pay respects at the grave site. Andrew was impressed with the fact that one man could so positively affect so many.

***

Andrew and Amy worked hard, all through the school years. Maybe it was the fact that they stayed busy most of the time. But for whatever reason, they didn't seem to mind the time spent at school. Amy became involved in Andrew's studies and Andrew assisted Amy in some of the problems of work. The experience brought them closer and closer together.

Angels

"Andrew absorbs his earthly learning well, both in school and in life, and consistently seeks ways of understanding the relation of these facts to his life."

"Yes, he does keep these theories and teachings in the proper position of importance, unlike some who use this partial knowledge to completely direct their lives."

"To many, this organized study of earth's facts is a complete enlightening. But, of course, that is based on earthly standards."

"Of course, if that is all you have accepted, then that is the end result. The end."

***

Andrew does continue to question and so continues to learn.

Chapter 5
Four Long Years Later

"Andrew...Andrew...you did it! You got your degree!"

"Yeah, feels good. Thanks to you baby, really feels good. Couldn't have done it without you."

"Well, you worked, too."

"Sure, but I know it wouldn't have happened without your help! Did I mention I appreciate it and how much I love you."

"Um, tell me about it later."

"Promise!"

"Now Mr. College Degree man, what you gonna do now?"

"You mean after we celebrate? I...didn't want to think about that right now. At least not right now – today."

"What's the matter, Andrew?"

"Well, it takes some think'un, as always. You know my old friend Uncle Ben told me once when we were fish'un, and some how we were talking about school and all, and well, he said, 'An education is like a fancy rod and reel. If you use it right, you can catch more fish and have more fun than ever before. If you don't, it will just cost you money. The rod and reel don't catch the fish, you do!'"

"You got something big bothering you, haven't you?"

"Amy...Amy baby I can't hide anything from you, can I?"

"No you can't, Andrew Brown. Somethun's been bothering you for some time now. And I think it's time you talk to me about it."

"Yeah, you're right. Where'd you get that crystal ball, anyway?"

"It's a secret."

"OK, but hey, listen. It is time to celebrate. Let's go to that

87

place in town we went to that time, Raymond's. Kinda reminds me of Shurpes only it costs more and the food ain't as good and it's newer and that name reminds me of that big meat head I used to have to spar with all the time, back in that other life. Other than that it's a great place. They take checks."

"Raymond's! Yeah, like you say...other than...you got to stand in line. But OK we're celebrating. Lets go."

***

"Aw, well, now Andrew, look at this. We get to sit by the window and people watch – not so bad."

"I thought the people were watch'un us. Gee, I might want to hold your hand or somethun."

"Well this way you'll just have to behave yourself."

"Seems like I been do'un an awful lot of that lately. Maybe we could expand our celebration a little."

"You just cool it. I'll celebrate with you, all you want, later. Right now, you and I are go'un to have a little talk, You got somethun on your mind and I want to hear about it."

Andrew looks at Amy. Funny how so many memories can go through your mind in just seconds.

"Aw, Am, I don't know where to start. I feel like I want to say, 'I want to think about it.' And yet I know you could easily say 'You've had four years,' and I guess you could add in a lot of sleepless nights. But those four years always seemed to be in a big rush to get something done. I don't know where they went. Also I don't want to lay around and be think'un forever. And I do need to make that buck now and then. And also I know I don't want to jump into the first thing I see, and then get tied up in that, and just stay and stay; when it's not really what I want to do."

"Honey, my crystal ball is clearing up a little bit and I haven't lived with you for four years without learning to read you pretty good. I don't think your go'un to make any heavy decisions right here, right now.

"I have a suggestion. I have some vacation time coming and I don't care if you even quit that box-stacking job. Andrew, let's go see my mother. Now wait a minute. She's by herself now. I could help her and visit. And we could have some time together. OK, lots of time – just us. She lives by the river!"

"You...you, Amy you ...you cover all the gaps, don't ya? By the river, huh?"

"OK, so I am trying to talk you into it. But we both deserve a break. It would be fun. And maybe you could think things out, down by the river. Lets make it two weeks."

"By the river, huh!? Aw, me. What can I say? Let's do it!"

At Amy's Mother's House

Andrew and Amy drive down to her mother's house. Not much of a place – on the outskirts of a small town in southern Illinois. Amy's mother is in bad health. Has trouble getting around. It's good that Amy can be there and help her out.

They receive a truly genuine welcome and prepare to settle in for a few relaxing days in the place of Amy's youth and in the company of her mother. Amy gives Andrew a personal tour of all her favorite spots.

One day they follow a little path through the garden and past a couple of cherry trees that leads to an open area right by the river. It's a much traveled path for Amy. She came here many times while growing up. There's still an old wooden bench there. It kinda leans against a big old elm tree right on the bank of the river.

In early July Amy used to walk through the patches of raspberries that grew wild along one side of the path toward the end, picking some, and blend them with some black cherries from the two trees by the garden. The combination of the two, she thought, made an unusual and delicious treat.

Eating berries and cherries and sitting and thinking by the river Amy seemed to find the best times in her early life. It was here she worked out the many problems that seemed to bother her then. And here she dreamed and planned a future life. Here also she dreamed of the wonderful person she would share the rest of her life with. Later she wondered if that dream would ever really happen. And now, now she was bringing the man of her dreams to share her own personal and secret place...by the river.

Amy's Spot

"Sure you know where your go'un, Babe?"

"Oh yes, I'm sure. It may be a little overgrown but you might say I've been here before."

"Am I seeing water through there?"

"Oh, yes, you'll see it in a minute. We'll be right by the water."

"Well that kinda takes me back. Used to be an ole water man myself."

"So I've heard. It was part of the bait, ya know."

"Oh yeah, I'm beginning to understand you – a little after all this time."

"Just so you don't get too smart."

"No danger."

***

"Here we are...."

"You bring your old boy friends here?"

"I never brought anybody here!"

"Um, nice. Looks like the ole Mississ'sip hasn't changed much. Just as muddy look'un as it ever was."

"Looks better at night. - With a moon. Maybe I can get you back here then. You relate to moonlight on the Mississippi?"

"You got to be kid'un."

"Well, seems like 'Ole Man River' is some sorta part of both our lives."

"Guess so. Gotta admit, something relaxing about it, dirty as it is."

"What did you think about on the river."

"Oh, day dreamed, or night dreamed about all kinda of things. One of the things is still a bit of a puzzle, I guess. I used to just look at the water and the sky and the world and all, and wonder what's it all about. Kinda where I am now, I guess. That box'un thing's over. But what?"

"I know. I used to think I wanted to do something that would make me feel good and maybe even make other people feel good, too. I didn't know what. I used to take care of stray animals. Drove my folks crazy. Made me get rid of them. I felt sorry for them.

"I remember the boys used to put baby kittens in a sack with a rock and throw them in the river. An old lady down the road gave them a quarter to get rid of a litter one time. I cried."

"I can understand. I had an old dog once. Just a mut. In fact I called him 'ole mut.' It seems like he actually knew what I was thinking. Sometimes, in the summer, he'd just start kinda whin'un. And I used to say he wants to go the river. An' when I'd get up and start...he'd get all excited. My mother said I used it as just an excuse to go down to the river again. Maybe so."

"Back to human be'uns...just what is eat'un on you, anyway, all this time?"

"Well, it's....Hey what was that? That your mama?"

"Oh, it's Annie May from next door. What's the matter!?"

"Amy! Sorry to bother. I thought I'd find you down here. It's your mama. She fell down. But it's OK. I helped her up and she's fine. She wanted me to fetch you. Better go."

"Thank you, Annie May. I'm go'un. Come on, Andrew. Oh, Annie May, this is my husband, Andrew Brown."

"Oh, your husband? Andrew – *Brown*? Pleased to meet you. You two better run along now. I'll talk to you later."

Amy and Andrew go back to the house. Amy's mother is all right, but gave Amy a scare anyway and she spent the rest of the day close to her. Her mother said she was glad she was there. Everything was OK, but it made Amy think about how it would be if something did happen to her mother and how good it was to be able to be there, help her mother and enjoy her stay. After Amy fixes supper and helps her to bed, she and Andrew decide to take another stroll to the river, by moonlight.

"Your mom ever do that before?"

"Oh, yeah! Couple times. It's her hip and legs. Doctor says she has a strong heart, especially for someone at her age. I guess women have less heart trouble than men. Seems like anyway. She's OK now that she's in bed. She'll be fine. 'Course it bothers me anyway when she falls. I gave her her pills. She'll sleep."

"OK to leave her then?"

"Oh yeah, I wouldn't leave if it wasn't. She'll probably sleep till 8 or 9 in the morning. Say, I think where we left off, you were about to answer my question."

"Right, tough question to answer altogether. Takes a little explaining."

"I'm listening, we got time. Mama's OK."

"Kinda hard to know where to start. You know I'm always questioning everything, life – everything. Again, it's like my ole grandma used to say. I was born with one foot in the river and the other in Missouri. You know, the 'show me' state. I always thought I had to know how everything works and why. Well, somewhere along the line I realized that I'm just not going to know exactly how everything works. I think nobody will, but I think I've kinda got everything straight as far as I'm concerned.

"I know I couldn't be satisfied with my life work'un in that warehouse or in the soy bean mill like Bo does. Nothing wrong with it. It's good for Bo. It just isn't for me. I guess we thrashed that all out four years ago. But I still have a problem.

"Amy, ya know when I was a kid we had gangs. Like now, I guess. Anyway, one time a kid I knew in one of the gangs beat up a kid in the other. So the other gang decided to get even. They caught the kid in front of a restaurant on a side street. Streets were paved with bricks then. This one, anyway. They knocked him down and then they got one on each arm and one on each leg and lifted him up and slammed him down on the brick street several times. People who saw it said his head flopped around like a rag doll. I know his head hit the bricks so hard it killed him. Right there.

"When I got there his mother was sit'un in the street with her son's bloody head in her lap, cry'un her eyes out. She kept say'un 'why, why, why does this have to happen?'

"You know Am, that made a terrible impression on me. I don't think I'll ever forget that night. It's kinda been on the back burner in my mind, like they say ever since, even though I'm into other things at the time."

"You never told me that before."

"I know. Reason I'm tell'un you now is, it kinda helps explain what's on my mind, I think."

"That would make an impression, although I don't think there's much you can do to change that."

"Maybe not that exactly. I can't bring Kenny back or anything. But, I am wondering if there's something I can do to keep such things from happening again."

"Um...um...that's a tall order."

"I know. That's why it takes a lot of think'un. An' that's why I have to share it with you. You know the other thing...."

"What?"

"Well you've met Bo and Nell and Lori and well, when I was in their house back home, Bo told Nell that I was responsible for them be'un there. 'Cause I pulled him out of the river one time. I guess I did, but it made me feel strange, him say'un if it wasn't for me they wouldn't be there. And then I got to think'un again. Suppose it was, well nobody knows what heaven's like or anything about it, really. But suppose you were there, where ever it is and somebody said, 'I wouldn't be *here* if it wasn't for you.' How would that made you feel? Or if someone wasn't there because of you!?

"Um, Andrew you *do* think of some things. An' I'm think'un on what you just said. Gotta let that sink in a little."

"I know. Say that's an awful pretty moon on the river. Maybe that's enough heavy talk for one night."

"Um, yeah, well maybe so. Wanta go for a swim?"

"Well now. That is a change! A, really doesn't look like this is a good place for a swim."

"Not here. I'll show you. Down here a little ways. There's some backwater. Nobody can see you in the daylight, let alone at night."

"Really. Sounds great. Let's go."

For quite a while Amy and Andrew have a great moonlight swim. Amy has intentionally postponed the rest of their little talk. She is having a little "back burner' action of her own. She and Andrew have been together too long and too close not to have an idea of what is going on in his mind. Just have to be sure about these things and run them through the old mind machine enough times to be sure <u>sure</u> of the way you want to go. And the way that is best.

Next Morning

"Morning Mama, how you do'un this morning?"

"Oh I'm just fine, Amy. My old legs just give out on me at times. I didn't tell you before because it wasn't for sure, but Annie May is going to move in with me. She's have'un trouble make'un the rent on her place and this one's all paid for, so she's just go'na move in here. Then she can pick me up when I fall down."

"I hope that won't be too often, but sounds like a good arrangement to me. You can help each other that way and you'll have some company."

"I think it'll be all right. We been together a long time,

94

friends and all. Ain't no reason to try to keep up two places. Say, you two go down to the "bench" last night? Better watch out 'bout that place. It'll get ya."

"Mama, what you talk'un 'bout?"

"That's a powerful place down there and there's a full moon out too. It'll 'tetch' ya. Ya know your father proposed to me sit'un right there in that old bench. 'Course it was new then. An' with a full moon and all - 'course you already done that. But you better watch out."

"Why, Mama, I didn't know that. All the times I used to go there. You never told me."

"Aw child, I don't tell you everything. Got to keep some things for myself."

"I can't believe that...all those years. I must have inherited the love of that place."

"Heh! Maybe so. Well, you two go on down there tonight. It usually does good things – usually."

"Well, Mrs. Brown we might just do that. Need all the help I can get sometimes."

Amy and Andrew take Mrs. Brown's advice and return to the "'bench" again that night.

"You know Andrew, I can't get over the thing Mama told me about this place. It makes me think. She and my dad walked this way and.... Funny how a place can have such an effect on you."

"Well, if you jumped in the river and floated on down a few miles, you'd come to the place I used to go. My folks never were there, but I sure spent a lot of time there. Know what you mean."

"You know, know'un that kinda puts me in a mood. This always was 'my' spot. But now I'm share'un it with you and I feel like my mom and dad are share'un it with me. Strange."

"Um, yeah."

"Andrew I been share'un a *lot* of other thoughts too, privately, since last night. I cut you off because I had to think...You try'un to tell me you want to work for the church?"

"Amy... you always just straighten things right out, don't you? Well, I think the answer is 'yes'. But I just don't know how or what. I'm still asking myself questions and I'm not trained to do that sorta thing."

"I didn't let you finish last night. You let it all out?"

"I guess you got the punch line but...I started to tell you about my friend there and his mother. It haunted me, about her questions and mine, too. Why does this happen and more important, how can this be avoided so it don't happen again? There's only one way. There's not enough police or laws or anything else to completely control it. People just have to be raised to know the right way and why it's best. And I guess I just can't turn my back on it and say that's their problem. First of all, it's not just their problem, it's *our* problem, and it affects us all. I tried finding my place, boxing and all. Didn't work. Somebody should have beat the stuff'un out of me sooner, but then I learned a pretty good lesson. Sorry someone else had to suffer for it.

"As far as God is concerned, well I thought about that most of all. Simple answer is...first, like your grandpa said, just has to be. Something had to be there always. That's it; that's God! Think of all the things in this world, real, abstract, everything. Anybody who thinks about it seriously, with an open mind, can't come to any other conclusion. Second, there's the other side of it. It's not a matter of me making up my mind to do something. It's – I can't stand doing anything else. It's like standing by the river and watching someone drowning and doing nothing about it. But I can't ask you to...."

Amy puts up that same finger she put up four years ago.

"You! What do I have to do, ask you to marry me all over again? We're not two people. We're one! You go; we go. You got it this time, Mr. Brown? Ummmmm... Speaking of go'un, want to go swimming?"

"Ummm yourself! Twist my arm

About Angels

Hard to explain, like, we're created in God's image, spiritually. So also are Angels. They not only have free will but also feelings and emotions. If you wanted to explain their actions right now, you could say they were looking on and smiling. Not about the swimming; it's OK for married people, but about Andrew and Amy's decision.

***

Amy and Andrew stay a few more days with her mother. Helping Annie May move in and being satisfied that everything is going to work out well for her mother and Annie May. Plans for their new future turn out to be more involved than they thought at first. Main thing is... Andrew has decided to enter the seminary.

The how, where and when are all things that have to be decided. It was not a big thing to quit his job at warehouse. But since they had to move, Amy had to leave the hospital where she had worked into a good position she had been trying to reach a long time. But, this was their firm decision and, they felt, their destiny

Angels Again
(Later)

"Seems strange that Andrew has to go through such a long procedure and spend so much of their time to gain the information that could be transferred so easily."

"Remember he's of that world; we're of this one."

"I know, but I have heard, even in that world, 'nothing's impossible.'"

"But I don't think *anyone* in their earth world has reached that stage yet. But he can help us and himself with some of the people he will be associated with."

"I know, and he is approaching one such situation now."
"Let us observe."

At the Seminary

After two years at the seminary, as happens to all seminary students, Andrew is assigned to intern duty at a church in the synod for a year of real life experience, being exposed to the duties and problems of the church as it really is. He is assigned to St. Mark's. It is a small, rather old church not too far from the seminary. As he progresses through the year, the presiding pastor, Pastor John Edmonton, guides him and little by little gives him more responsibility in the work of the church. It's the latter part of the year and Pastor John is on vacation.

"Well, Am, I guess I have to go see that old Mrs. Jacobson I've heard about. She's on her deathbed in the hospital with terminal everything I guess. They say she's difficult to deal with. Long time church go'er, but questions everything and has no family, few friends, and lost her alcoholic husband years ago."

"Just hold her hand and pray with her. Isn't that what you're supposed to do?"

"Sure, that's easy. But you know I keep thinkin. Is that really what she needs or wants? Oh, I'm not putting prayer down.... I guess I'm just think'un too much again. Guess I'll just have to see what happens."

At the Hospital

"Good morning Mrs. Jacobson. I'm Andrew Brown from St. Mark's. Pastor John is on vacation. I came over to see how you are and if I could do anything for you...."

"They take care of that here. I know you, black boy. What do you think you can do?"

"Actually I'm not quite sure at this time, but that's part of what I came to find out. I do represent someone who does have the power to do a lot...."

"I wish I could believe that."

"They tell me you're a long time church member. What is it that really bothers you?"

Mrs. Jacobson stares at Andrew...for quite a while.

"I told you...."

"You mean really believing? I can understand that. I had to face that myself"

"It's easy for you. They tell me I'm going to die."

"I had to satisfy myself, too. Do you mind if I share some of my thoughts with you? I'm not tiring you, am I?"

"No."

"I'm sure this sounds like an odd thing to talk about but this is my prescription for you. You have to take it daily and let it work. It took me years. So you have to really think on it, OK?"

"Yes."

"Mrs. Jacobson, salvation the Good Lord takes care of. But, believing – you have to do. I said I know where you are because I've been there myself. And I have. You have to have something to base your belief and your faith on. Think on this. Scientists don't know how the world started. Probably never will. But this I know by logic. In the beginning something had to be there always. Had to be. Can't start something from nothing. No other way. That something is God. Think about it. Now, the next step is a little harder, but it can be done. Again *you* have to do it. Think about all the things in this world. Everything you know. Think how they work. Things you can touch and things you can't. Especially things you can't, you know what I mean? Think on it with an open mind. No one involved in this but you.

One other thing, an unbeliever friend of mine said, 'If there was a God why wouldn't He come to this world and show Himself and do something to prove He *was* God and *do* something to help us. Isn't that what Jesus did? Mrs. Jacobson

I certainly will pray for you and I'll be back tomorrow. You think on this till then. Rest now. I'll see you tomorrow."

Back Home

"Well Am, I think I'm probably going to hear about this one. I didn't exactly follow Pastor John's instructions. 'Don't get too heavy. Pray for them. Don't tire them out'."

"Why? What happened?"

"Aw, you know how I feel about just going through the motions and being sure to say the right and acceptable thing and all. And I'm not trying to be Mr. Know It All. But dog gone it, I can't help but feel I just have to try to get down to the source of the real problem. I said to myself, 'what good does it do to hold her hand and pray when she tells me she's not sure there's a God'! The thoughts raced through my mind! What do I tell her, the Bible says so? She's heard that. Am, I think she's one of those realist, material type of people who needs something... something she can understand and accept. She's missed something, somewhere. I'm trying to find it, and *I'm* do'un the pray'un for the Good Lord to help *me* help her. I know I'm out on a limb; it's actually scary. I hope I'm do'un the right thing! God help me! I hope I'm do'un the right thing!"

Angels

"Your doing the right thing Andrew, and we're here to help you."

Hospital
(Next Day)

"Oh, you the chaplain to see Mrs. Jacobson?"

"Yes, I'm the intern from St. Mark's filling in for Pastor Edmontson."

"Well, maybe you better go right in. Make it short. She's not doing real well right now."

"Thank you. Good morning, Mrs. Jacobson. I'm glad to see you. How are you today?"

"I thought about...what you told me."

"Good...."

"I've – got – something – for – you. You got me started – on the – right way. Now – you listen. Something else – made me believe. You had to be sent here, you know, to find me. Where I was – I'm not there anymore. I got a – lot of help, in the night. I'm all right now. God bless *you*, son."

Mrs. Jacobson didn't say anymore. She died in the early hours the next morning.

At Home

"Amy, I tell you something. That was an experience. Mrs. Jacobson did more for me than I could ever do for her. You know, they said she seemed comfortable after that. Can you believe it? I know one thing. When she said 'God bless *you*, son' she moved her hand over to mine and gave me a little squeeze. I didn't know there could be so much feeling in a little squeeze from an old lady."

"You know, Andrew it makes me feel good when you tell me things like that. And the odd thing about it is it seems to bring us closer together. You know, I'm not sure I really accept such things, but sometimes I could almost believe some guardian angel or something pushed you into me back there in Chicago and spilled my milk and eggs. I sure didn't think so at the time!"

"No, I didn't either. You know what I think about? Long time ago, somewhere, I heard 'God doesn't change things; He changes people and they change things!' I don't know if I *completely* agree, but well, could it be possible that God or His angels use us to accomplish His work here? Could it have happened with Mrs. J....That's kinda hard to believe....What am I say'un?

Angels

"I think the earth people would be greatly surprised if they knew how much their lives are influenced by what they simply call 'guardian angels!'"

"Yes, what a, what do they call it, 'over simplification.' If they only would seek the real answers they *would* be surprised."

"That is true. And we have some 'guardian angel' work to do right now."

"I know. I think Andrew has been strengthened by this experience also."

(Later)

Andrew went on to complete his study and work through the seminary. He was ordained and went to a position immediately as an assistant pastor in the old church where he had spend his internship, St. Mark's.

He was remembered there and had a lot of close friends. Also he had made a very good impression on the people of that congregation. He fit right in and soon gained a reputation – well deserved.

One afternoon after some time of satisfying and rewarding work at St. Mark's, Pastor John called Andrew into the church office.

"Andrew, I can't tell you how much you have helped me and many other people here at St. Mark's. As happens so often when you do a good job at something, you are moved to something bigger and better because of it. I have been asked to recommend you for an opening in a larger church as their full time and only pastor. As much as I would hate to see you leave

St. mark's I could do no other than to recommend you very highly. Of course this is far from final. Trinity, a larger church up north will, I'm sure, consider several people. But I think your chances are very good. Again understand this is not final by any means, But I thought you should know you are being seriously considered."

Andrew is elated. He does have some mixed emotions about leaving the position at St. Mark's. He has experienced a life more than he had any idea existed, through the warm, friendly, completely satisfying feeling he has known in seeing the lives of real people being changed and helped. And he has been a part of it. It's one of those 'you have to go through it yourself things'. You cannot express it fully. You have to live it to know it. Yes, it has to be a "been there – done that" thing to completely appreciate it. It has overwhelmed Andrew. And again he has grown as a result of it.

***

Meanwhile the woman who is behind every successful man in this case is Amy. She is still working and working hard. At times conditions at Northside Hospital seem more than she can bear.

Amy has a patient on her hands who is "very critical." He is dying and he is very afraid and in very much pain – Mr. James.

"Amy! Oh, good heavens, glad I found you. Ole Chambers is having a snit. I answered your lights a couple times but she caught me do'un it. Can you get back out there?"

"Thanks, Joanie. I really appreciate it. I'll get out there, but I just can't leave him right this minute. Hope he'll drop off soon. He's got enough meds in him."

"OK, but don't stay too long."

"Nurse - nurse. You're not my nurse. Where's my nurse?"

"I'm you nurse for tonight Mr. James. I have been here before and I can help you. Do you need something now?"

"I don't know, everything's strange. You know about my

medicine? I need my medicine...."

"Yes, Mr. James. I gave it to you a little while ago. Remember? It'll work soon. You just lie back and relax."

"Oh nurse, nurse, I can't believe this. How'd I get here already. I'm not ready for this. Ole Father Time has picked my pockets. You understand? What's your name?"

"Amy. Amy Brown, Mr. James."

"Amy Brown, mind if I hold your hand?"

"'Course not. Better?"

Mr. James drops off to sleep.

***

"Well, there you are. Would you mind tending to the rest of the patients for a while? Instead of relying on the others of your shift to cover up for you."

"I'm sorry Mrs. Chamberlain, but I just couldn't leave him. He's in pain and he's scared to death he's going to die."

"Looks like he's sleeping peacefully to me. You better return to the desk and check your lights and finish your meds and charts. Then come to my office before you leave."

That Evening at Home

"Hi hon, didn't know you were home already."

"Took off a little early. Got some good news, I think. How was your day?"

"Well, glad you've got some good news. I'm afraid mine falls into the bad news category more than good. But, go ahead, tell me some good news first. Maybe it'll help me handle mine."

"Hey, babe. I'm sorry to hear you got bad news. Can I help you?"

"Sure, you can go ahead and tell me what your good news is."

"OK. Well, Pastor John called me into his office today and

said this large church up north, Trinity, has asked him to recommend me as a replacement, that is if I want to go, for their pastor who is leaving. He said that it's not final by any means, but he knows the pastor there and he thinks I have a good chance. Large church."

"Andrew! Andrew! Give me a hug. What is this? You know, that guardian angel's go'na have me believing in him yet."

"Him, huh? I thought it was a her."

"What ever."

"Say, what was it you were go'un to tell *me*?"

"Well, I know, like you said, we can't count our chickens yet, but I guess just the thought of it relieves me and makes me feel better anyway. You know that old Mrs. Chamberlain I'm always talk'un about, the head nurse, well, she got to me today, I guess. She called me in *her* office and started giving me a bad time about not having my charting done. 'Everybody's got theirs in but *you*, of course.' I asked her what she was talking about and she got real nasty. She said she wasn't going to give me any special privileges and I had to do my share like anyone else and bla - bla - bla. Anyway turns out, she got my charts mixed up with that pet of hers and she's the one who hadn't turned her charts in. But did she apologize? 'Course not! She said that wasn't the point, and that I couldn't expect any special favors being a minority.

"And then there was this old Mr. James, terminal patient, poor guy, he may not even make it through the night. Long story. I don't want to get into it. Anyway, I had just about had it today. I didn't know really what I wanted to do about it. But well, I guess you just put me in a better mood, even if nothing comes of it. It made me look past all this to what's more important."

"Oh, Amy! Mamy, this really brings it home to me. You carried the load long enough. No matter how this comes out I think we have to find a way to let you quite working. It's about time."

105

"Maybe we need another trip to mother's and another swim or two or three."

"Yeah, I do need to think this out. Oh, it's a great opportunity, and I appreciate it. I just am not completely sure it's for me or what I can handle. Only one way to find out, I guess."

***

Going to mother's was a little impractical at this time and they were quite a bit farther away than before. Anyway, Amy did quit her job soon afterwards and they turned their attention to the possible move for Andrew.

Angels

"It is quite comforting to work with Andrew and Amy. They are so receptive, even though they don't seem to accept it outwardly at times. Andrew has shown such a great change from the boy he was, questioning everything and living by the river in his youth. Now he's a mature adult, knowing the mission he wants to follow."

"Too bad more of the people there are not so. They are under a terrible negative influence. It is near impossible for them to overcome its forces by their powers alone!"

"Tragically that is true. We must follow Amy and Andrew now as they go to an even greater work. They will be united with others already working in the right direction and some still in a rather neutral position. Since Andrew and Amy are so receptive to aid, we will use them to guide others not so easily communicated with."

"Let us go now and continue with this growth."

Part II

Saul to Paul (?)

Chapter 1
Angels Meet "Near" Earth

"Things are certainly going well for Andrew and Amy. They are now going to be helpers with us trying to bring others into a higher level. Even though they are not aware of it."

"The others that you refer to are of a different attitude towards their existence here. Instead of a gradual growth from the beginning, they have gotten into a different mode. One which is harder to develop or change."

"Unfortunately this is true. They have decided, they have figured out the way. But have considered only that life. It puts them in a position of thinking they understand much. This makes them hard to change. Also they are not going to be influenced by people who they think are not as informed as they."

"You know this is one of the traps the other side uses to control people – the wrong way."

"Yes, and their traps must be full because it is a very clever finesse for the evil one. It uses their ego, as they say, to lead them astray."

"Indeed it does work well. We must use an even better way with a genuine and sincere approach to show them something beyond this temporal thing that they assume they have mastered."

"You realize the strongest and best thing in existence is love."

"Of course, it is boundless in all directions."

"Let us go then and see what is taking place."

Another Meeting - On Earth

Well, baby, this is it. What can I say? I finally got out of that rat hole. I'm moved in! Living in one of those neat neighborhoods with lawns and pools and all the good stuff. Georgia was OK, for a while, but what a pain! More headache than anything else anymore, and so much make-up...if it rained she'd melt.

Forty-eight and foot loose, man. The way I got it cut. I can hang it up at fifty-five.

I mean...this thing moves. What the...!? Stink'un woman drivers. You ought to be home raise'un kids or somethun. Stay in your own lane. Aw...man...now what? If your go'un to run the light - kick it! A... oh ... no... no!

Oh, you stupid woman! Now I'm going to hear - "You rear-ended me!" I'll rear end you! Aw, now look at this. She's going to ask me if I'm hurt. You want to see my driver's license?

"Oh, hello...I'm sorry I shouldn't have done that. I thought I could make the light and then I realized I couldn't...and with the rain and all. And I'm not used to this car yet. I'm sorry. Are you all right?"

"I'm OK, but I wonder about you."

"I'm fine, thank you. Is it too bad?"

"Well, let's take a look, OK? All right, all right, stop honk'un. Can't you see there's an accident here? Hum, well I guess I've seen worse."

"Oh good, I do hope it's nothing too bad."

"They're drive-able. Hey, look, it's rain'un. I'm get'un soaked and I'm tired have'un people honk at me. See that restaurant parking lot across the street? Think you can get over there? We'll exchange insurance company names over there. OK?"

"A yes, fine. I'll go over."

So They Go to the Parking Lot

*Oh - jeez she's a looker, but doesn't seem to be too bright.
Maybe I can talk her out of the whole darn thing. Might take a
little talking. Maybe I can buy her a cup of coffee or something.
I guess I can stand it that long*
"A, well, it's raining just as hard over here. Let's get out of
the darn rain. OK?"

"Sure, want to come in here?"

"A, no offense lady, but cars are kinda crowded and I can't
see to write anyway. Look, a – come on, I'll buy you a cup of
coffee. Let's go inside where it's dry, comfortable and we can
see. OK?"

"I think that's a good idea."

They Go to the Restaurant

"A, waiter, two. We just want a couple coffees. Yeah, this
is fine. A – have a seat. Well, I'm sorry I guess I don't even
know your name. I'm Paul Davies."

"Ann Winfield. Pleased to meet you."

"Yeah...same here. You...a...want a coffee or somethun?"

"Coffee's fine."

"Great. Two coffees, OK? A, well... Miss... a ... what was it,
Win...?"

"Winfield - Mrs. Winfield, I prefer Ann."

"Oh, sorry. A - Ann, looks like we're the victims of the
insurance companies!"

"Is that so? Why do you say that?"

"Well, you know how it goes. First, there's a big deductible.
Then your premium goes up forever. They get it all back from
you and more. You know, that's how they pay for those big
offices, etc. Insurance companies have all the money in this
country. Didn't you know that? That's the way it is."

"Are you suggesting we don't submit a claim?"

"Well, you know, wouldn't hurt to think it over, huh?"

"I suppose it wouldn't hurt to think it over, but at this point I'll have to tell you I'm in favor of notifying my insurance people."

"A, well, you know, there's no big hurry...."

"I suppose not but I do think we should exchange information at this time at least. Do you mind if I get your driver's license number etc.?"

"Oh, course not. Should do that."

"Here's my card. My driver's license number and car license number are on the back."

"Well yeah, I can give you my card and I'll write my driver's license and car license number on the back."

"Thank you."

"Ah - Ann Winfield, Oak Grov, ATTORNEY AT LAW. You're a lawyer!?"

"Yes, why, does that surprise you?"

"Oh no-o-o problem I, a, I mean I don't know you or anything. I had no idea you were a lawyer or attorney. Oh, here's the coffee. You a – take cream or anything?"

"Cream."

Oh, man, did I get shot down. Hey, how lucky can you get? Have to say this though...best look'un lawyer I ever saw. Man!

"Well, might as well finish our coffee. You – a – live around here?"

"Oak Grove."

"Oh, yeah, your card did say Oak Grove. You...have a family? You said Mrs. Winfield."

"Yes, I do. My husband died several years ago. I have a grown daughter. You?"

"I have a grown daughter also. She's in Ohio. And I've been divorced for a while. Your daughter must be too young to have any children of her own."

"Ha! Nice complement! No, not yet. You joined that club?"

"You mean grandparent? No, I'm afraid my daughter has

other things in mind."

"Well I guess I should be going. Sorry about your car."

"Oh I'm the one who should apologize. I ran into you after all. Hope you won't have any trouble getting it taken care of."

"I'm sure I won't."

"Well, if you – a – have any troubles let me know. I'd be glad to help you if I can."

"Thank you. That's nice of you. Bye bye."

"Bye.

Jeez - your tell'un a lawyer...if you have any trouble you'll help her. Ha...I got a full size color picture of you helping her. Hum...yeah, she is the best looking darn...or any other kind of lawyer or even an attorney I ever saw. Wonder what it's like talking to a lawyer all the time or even an attorney. Hum...wonder...jeez...she is a looker though. I guess a woman can be both good look'un and smart. Aw...well, better get out of here.

"Sir, sir, your wi – or a, your lady friend forgot her coat."

"Oh yeah...stopped rain'un. I guess she didn't miss it. Thanks."

Maybe I can catch her. - No use, she's gone. Better give it back to the guy in the restaurant. Well, no, maybe I'll keep it. Got her phone number. Maybe we can work something out. Well, I'll call her when I get home. Something about that babe. She just kinda haunts you.

Home .

Ah, let's see - where's the stink'un card? Ann Winfield, 276-7676. Well now ain't that classy. I guess lawyers can afford that.

"Oh, no! stink'un recorder. I hate those ever lov'un things, you...."

"Hello...."

"O – oh, hello! A – this Ann?"

"Yes, of course. What can I do for you?"
Jeez - don't throw me a line like that, honey."
"Why, ah, Ann you left you coat in the restaurant. I have it
and want to get it back to you. What's convenient for you?
Could I drop it off or maybe we could meet somewhere or
something?"
"Oh, you have it. Thank goodness. I noticed I didn't have it.
I didn't want to lose it. Thank you so much for calling."
"No problem."
"I don't want to put you to any trouble. I really appreciate
this. I do go through that same intersection almost everyday...."
"Great. That'll work. I usually go through there myself. No
trouble. Say, ah, that same restaurant? I'm good for another
coffee. If that's OK. What's a good time?"
"Well, I'm there around 6:30. However I can't do that until
Friday. Is that all right?"
"Oh sure, sure. Friday, 6:30. Same place. That's great."
"Good. Thank you again for taking care of it for me. I think
it could disappear if I left it in the restaurant and it's sort of a
keepsake. My daughter gave it to me. Thank you again and I'll
see you Friday."
"Right, Friday. That's great. OK!"
"Bye bye."
"Bye."

Friday

*I don't know what I'm do'un here. Some snooty dame cuts
me off in traffic and here I am waiting to meet her - and
plotting to buy her dinner - wait a minute - am I? Am I plotting
to but her dinner? This is the part that gets me. When I first
saw this babe I just wanted to tell her off and put her down,
and now I'm actually looking forward to seeing her.*
*And look at this. It's 6:35! Did you ever know a stink'un
woman to be on time? I suppose I'll get a page and a phone*

call now. "I've got a client - it's taking me longer than I thought."

I'm do'un her a favor - right? Ten minutes - ten minutes and I'm outta here - should make it five. I'm not....

"Oh hello Paul. Sorry I'm late. Would you believe - I got stuck in traffic. Story of my life, right? Been waiting long? Oh it's only 6:39. Well that's not bad."

"Hey, no problem. Nice to see you again. Have a seat. Hard day?"

"Well, as a matter of fact.... Hard day at the office I guess. One of those where everything does not go your way. I'm tired and...."

"Hungry?"

"Well yes, that too, I guess. Good place to be hungry. Are you having something?"

"Yeah, think I will. Hey, I know we just met and.... I hesitate to ask, but would you consider having dinner with me? Call it a peace offering for running into your car or – hey, just a friendship deal. You know I think I was a little short with you last time. I'm sorry. Dinner? Please?"

"Oh, really I couldn't impose...."

"No imposition. My pleasure. Let me insist. Please?"

"Well, that's nice of you and I am tired *and* hungry. But really I should at least pay my share. I should be thanking you. I do cherish that coat. It's just nice and cozy and as I told you, my daughter gave it to me."

"Oh, no problem. I, ah, didn't think it was a good idea to leave it here. Too tempting. A, let me suggest something."

Two Captain's Plate specials, and a little wine later and I'm in another world. Well maybe not another world but – what's happening here? Here I am sit'un here looking at this babe – or – lady and looking and thinking. There's something about her, you know? Sometimes you see someone who just stands out. She stands out. Really - has some sort of special personality. Something. Look at her. Either she is a wizard with make-up or she's the most natural beauty I ever saw. She's got to have make-up on, but you can't tell where it starts or stops. It looks like it's just her.

Besides that, in spite of the fact that at first I thought she was some kind of a feminist or something, now I find myself blabbing away, spilling my guts like I was talking to – to – oh, I don't know who. What's happening? The other weird thing, I don't want her to leave!! Jeez! Here I am scheming on a way to get together again and I – aw man – I don't know. What? Am I scheming on a way to get together again? No! No way. Well if that's not it – then WHAT?"

"Well, TGIF, huh? Do attorneys work on Saturday?"

"Oh, sure. Too often. Always some details to tie down etc. I'm sure I'm guilty of putting things off though the week to pick up on Saturday? You do that too?"

"Yeah, I'm always good at putting things off. I look forward to Sunday golf sessions. You golf?"

"I used to. Haven't in a long time."

"That's a shame. You shouldn't let the old golf clubs get rusty. Say I know we just sorta – ran into each other – ha. But, would you mind if I gave you a call sometime? Maybe try a little Sunday morning golf?"

"Sunday? Oh, it's been so long and I do teach a Sunday school class at 9:30. I...."

"Sunday school class!?"

Medium-Long Silence

"Oh come on, why does everyone seem so shocked when I tell them I teach a Sunday school class? Lots of people do."

"I'm sorry. I just didn't see you as a Sunday school teacher. I mean, that's good. I guess I just didn't think of lawyers and Sunday school teachers. Aw, gee, I'm get'un myself in trouble. Really, I think that's great. I guess I just don't know many Sunday school teachers – or lawyers. No offense. I just...."

"Don't worry about it. You're not the only one. I take a lot of flack at the office. I'm used to it. But I enjoy it and I think it's worth it. But...I do think I should be going...."

"I didn't mean to run you off...."

"No, no – no problem, But I really should go. Thank you again for dinner. It was very nice, and for taking care of my coat. I really do appreciate it."

"So-o-o-OK. My pleasure. A, is it OK, then, if I give you a jungle sometime – golf – somethun?"

Through a smile – "Sure –– bye bye."

"Bye."

Angels

"It's working - it's working"

Chapter 2
Glickmond-ology

Well, here it is Sunday morning golf and I'm doing it by myself, that is, unless that dizzy Glickmond shows up. I don't know if I can put up with his drivel or not. But, then when could I ever.

Awe, man, here he comes. If he says, "Match you for a Mary," I'm going to puke. Look at the pants on that turkey. Wonder who he took those away from.

"Hey, Paul. Match you for a Mary!"

"Jeez, Glick, you got a one track mind. Don't you ever think of anything else?"

"Sure, sexy woman, big cars, lots of money. What's eat'un you anyway?"

"Nothing!"

"Oh yeah? Well, heads or tails?"

"Awe, shut up. Go get two. You owe me anyway."

"OK, OK, I'm go'un. What a sweetheart you are this AM."

"So go."

***

"OK, you got it. I hope this juice works miracles on your pain in the neck attitude. What's eat'un you anyway? I thought you got everything squared away. You and your ex still chip'un."

"None of your business. Drink up."

"OK, you go'un to play any golf this morning, Mr. Davies or are you going to sit there and be obnoxious all day?"

"Come on, let's go."

***

"Oh, into orbit – nice slice. You got a homing device on that baby?"

"Hey, knock it off, will ya Glick? I've had it!"

"Look, Pauly baby, I've had it too. I think you better get a little attitude adjustment. The bar stools are just behind those trees over there. Lets go wet our snoots. I'll even let you buy."

"Oh, what the...c'mon. I'll match ya."

***

"Well, Pauly-wauly what's the sweat? Tell ole Glick all about it. I thought you got Georgia out of your life for good. She want more money again?"

"Nah, nah. That's settled."

"Well, what do I get, three guesses...or what?"

"Awe, I don't know. It's hard to explain. Long story...."

"Cheez, we got a get a designated driver?"

"Hey, you ever have any serious thoughts or do they give you headaches?"

"OK, OK. You don't have to get nasty. Go ahead, I'm listening."

"Actually I don't know how to say it. Big problem is, I can't even understand it myself."

"Well now. How do we handle things like this? How about starting from the beginning?"

"Ha, yeah. OK. Here goes. I'm come'un home the other night. Rain'un like crazy. Anyway, I rear end this gal in a fancy BMW. She cuts me off, OK? Right way I'm ticked. So we go to this restaurant to exchange info and stuff. Get out of the rain, ya know. Well, we have a cup and I find out she's a lawyer."

"Oh man! She suing you? Go see big John McKinner. I suppose she's claiming whiplash."

"No, no. Wait a minute. That's not it at all. If your gonna listen, just listen, OK?"

"All right already. Ya dry?"

"No, but go on. Get it."

"OK, I'm back. So you ran into this babe. She's a lawyer and drive'un a big BM."

"Yeah, but that's really got nothing to do with it. Well yeah, it has - but, anyhow she leaves her coat in the restaurant."

"I'm be'un patient."

"I keep the coat."

"All right!"

"No, wait a minute. I keep it for her. I call her up and tell her I've got it, OK? Well, anyway we meet in the same restaurant, so I can give it back to her and I buy her dinner...."

"...You run into her car. You steal her coat and you buy her dinner. Yeah, you're mixed up OK. But, go ahead, I'm listening."

"Aw man! It's got nothing to do with any of those things. I mean really."

"OK."

"Look, while we're having dinner and a glass of wine...."

"Wine!?"

"Hey, anyway, while we're talking back and forth and I'm look'un at her and everything. Well I don't know. Glick, I just enjoyed it. I didn't want her to leave. And oh yeah, she's a Sunday school teacher."

"What!? Pardon me while I choke. You are mixed up! BMW, a lawyer, ya rear ended her, stole her coat and now you tell me she's a Sunday school teacher. Next you'll tell me she's a looker!"

"As a matter of fact...."

"OK, I think I'm beginning to get the picture. You don't know whether to get a lawyer, fall in love or mess around, right?

"Two out of three ain't bad. But wait a minute, you don't know this mixed up feeling I got. I never felt this way before."

"Yeah, well maybe so, but I'll tell you what. Ole Glick's got some advice for you. You never felt like this before. Well I never saw you so screwed up before. Whichever one of the two it is, you got to get it out of your head. So call the babe, go see her, get this done one way or the other, cause I ain't put'un up with you whin'un any longer. Hey, I gotta go. See ya later. Do it!"

Old Glick is such a jerk most of the time, but underneath it all he does come up with some straight shots once in a while. He's right.

Chapter 3
They Meet Again

They come together again (the angels that is) and again observe the events of earth.

"Interesting to notice how things develop. The inhabitants of this earth have been given the gift of complete freedom in their lives...yet they can be influenced from the outside."

"And as we observed before...it is needed when they are overpowered by those *wrong* influences from the outside. And they seem so attracted by them."

"Indeed these influences have been very strong here. Much too strong. Of course, that's why we're here."

"You know we must use the existing material things and other people of earth to guide them."

"Except in extreme circumstances."

"Of course. Like bales of hay?"

"It *was* necessary."

"Yes, and if you are thinking of this influence on others...it has already started. As for these two...it has only been indirectly...so far. But that will change."

Golf Conference - On Earth

Paul's House

276-7676 – *oh, no, that stink'un recorder again. Bah I don't want to talk to that thing. Yeah...beep...a...this....*

"Hello."

"Oh! Oh hello, Ann. A, Ann this is Paul – Paul Davies. How ya do'un?"

"Why I'm fine."

"Hope I'm not interrupting anything?"

"Not at all."

"Well, a, Ann, you remember the other night we talked about a little golf? Well I wonder if we could do that, say some Sunday PM. I guess that wouldn't conflict with your Sunday school class, would it?"

"No, not in the afternoon, no."

"Great! A, this Sunday, maybe?"

"Well, this is a coincidence! I mentioned before I hadn't played in a long time and now I have two opportunities at the same time. I am playing with a couple of friends. Would you like to join us? We could make it a foursome? They're nice people."

"Oh sure, that would be great. Two?"

"As a matter of fact that would work just fine. Do you mind just meeting us there? I'm meeting them just outside the coffee shop. In fact, the Espresso Shop, it is now, I guess. We would meet inside, but we wanted to play first. That OK?"

"Sure, sure, Ann. That's fine. Two-o'clock, coffee shop or make that Espresso Shop. That's great, great. See you there then."

"OK, Paul. Bye bye."

Hum - I wanted her all to myself. But, I didn't want to kick an opportunity. And, well I guess I can't be too picky at first anyway. At first!? Well, anyway I'm committed now.

Sunday Morning

Awe, man, Sunday morning is bad enough. Now no golf, and this thing this PM, I don't know. I almost wish I'd said no. What the hey! I can't let this gal start leading me around, start – what am I saying. What makes me think I'm starting something?

Aw – stink'un phone. Who'd be calling me Sunday morning?

"Hello, course it's me. Ya dialed this number didn't cha? Hey, what da you mean, where am I? Three guesses, turkey. I ain't married to you, ya know. I didn't want to play. OK? No, I ain't sick. I'm play'un this PM. *We* aren't play'un. I'm play'un with Ann. Yeah, she's the one. Yeah, yeah – Ann. Aw, but out Glick. Go chop up some grass somewhere. Ga bye."

That flip flop, what does he think? I gotta report to him every Sunday morning. Next thing you know he'll be wanting a full report on the romance in my life or something. Wouldn't take long. Well, guess I'll get my S,s done, look for something appropriate to wear this PM and – hey, I wonder who we're playing with? Probably some ex boy friend and his wife or something. And they won't know diddely about golf.

PM

OK. Here I am. Coffee shop, 2 PM. So where is she? Don't tell me this is one of those dames who can't be anywhere on time.

"Oh, hello Paul. Sorry we're late...."

"Not Ann's fault. I'm afraid it was us who caused the delay...."

"Oh no, anyway it's only 2:11. Paul, I want you to meet two newly acquainted but very good friends of mine. Meet Pastor Andrew Brown and this is Mrs. Brown, Amy. This is my friend, Paul Davies."

More than a Medium-Long Silence

Pastor – pastor – like in preacher. I don't believe it. I - I - I - yi - yi...."

"Oh, a, pleased to meet you, Pastor and Mrs. Brown. You from around here?"

"Well actually we're from southern California, recently. But, of course, we're considering moving here. I guess that's what we are going to chat about while pretending to play golf with Ann. You a member of Trinity also?"

"Trinity?"

"No, Paul's just a friend of mine. I hoped you wouldn't mind if we made it a foursome."

"No, no that's fine. Maybe Mr. Davies and I can find something to talk about while you and Andrew talk church business."

Holy Moses, I'm going to small talk with this babe while my golf date talks church with some preacher. Man, what's this chic got me into?"

"I'm sorry Paul, I guess I do owe you an explanation. You see, Pastor Brown here is being considered as the new pastor of our church, now that Pastor Moore is leaving. The church always interviews a new replacement quite thoroughly before making a decision. And I understand that Pastor Brown needs some more insight and time to be sure he's making the right move. Am I right, pastor?"

"Yes, Ann, I'm sorry to be so much trouble and I want to emphasize that I do appreciate the consideration from a church like Trinity. But, well, it's hard to explain, but this is a big step in my life...."

"I understand Pastor. I think everyone agrees and thinks it is better for both of us to be sure it's the right thing."

"Well, thank you. By the way Paul, I want to thank you for letting us but into your golf game with Ann today. She said she was sure you wouldn't mind. I hope that's true."

"Oh sure, sure. No problem. Glad to have you."

Now that's weird. He's saying she had the date with me first. But, on the phone she said she already was playing with them!?"

9th Hole

"Ah, that was great. Relaxing. Ann, you have made me feel

126

better about the whole thing. And Paul, the ultimate in making someone feel comfortable, is to let them win at golf. Thank you. Hate to leave such good company but we do have two meetings yet with the church people. Can't be late. I think we'll have to skip the coffee. Paul, certainly enjoyed meeting you. Hope to see you in the future. Ann, thank you again and we'll see you tonight."

"Thank you Pastor. Bye bye."

"Paul, I'm sorry, I guess I wasn't very friendly and I apologize. Hope you can understand. This is most important for me and for us and for Pastor Brown too, I guess. Can I make it up to you? How about that coffee? You interested?"

"Sure, and I'm going to hold you to that 'make it up to you' part. You'll have to play me another time, or maybe dinner? I don't like being taken on the course. Hey, you play a mean game."

"Thanks. I used to play with my Dad. He's a sore loser. Paul, you're a good sport to put up with all that talk. I'm sure it was foreign to you. I'm sure you couldn't know what's going on in our church or even know Pastor Brown and his wife. I guess I do owe you at least an explanation. It was nice of you to invite me to golf with you. I know I took advantage and I guess I fibbed a little. I told you I was playing with someone when I talked to you, and I hadn't even asked them yet. But, I knew I wanted to do that and I just hoped it would work out. I...."

"Aw, hey, don't worry about it. I enjoyed it. Tell me, I was talking to Mrs. Brown – Amy – and she says the preacher, or pastor is having a hard time making up his mind about accepting this call? You mean the church is having trouble deciding whether to hire him or not and he's having trouble trying to decide whether he wants to be their preacher or not?"

"Yes. That's about it. It's a long story, or at least a complicated one. You see the church has been going through a long struggle trying to stay alive, let alone grow. And the pastor has received another call that he thinks is right for him, and the church members think they need some new blood to give the church a boost. Pastor Brown has a big decision to make also. First, of course, he'll be the first black pastor of an all white church."

"Well, I guess that would stir things up. What do they do, take a vote or something?"

"Yes, in the end they do, but first in this case it's up to Pastor Brown to decide if this is what he thinks is best for him and for the church."

"I heard that line about how he was a professional fighter once, until he literally got it pounded into his head that boxing was not what he wanted to do with his life. Kinda well put, huh?"

"Yes, according to what he has told me he has made some important and difficult decisions in his life, and he feels that he must make the most of what he has decided to do. It's like they say at church, He feels he has a 'call', a strong one. As you can tell, he has some definite ideas about things."

"He sure does. But, what's your part in this?"

"Well I'm chairman of the Board of Parish Education and part of our function is the responsibility of proper Christian education in the church, like Sunday school, vacation bible school and the general teaching and education of the people at church. So I am naturally concerned about a new pastor, although it's not directly our responsibility, as a committee, to select one. More than that, I have a deep interest in the workings of the church. It's everything. Also I was the first to meet Pastor Brown and Mrs. Brown. Mostly because I was available to go and talk to them when he was a possible new pastor at our church. As I got to know him, I became convinced he is the person we need to lead us in our church."

"Wow, this is all pretty heavy for me. I guess I'll have to confess I don't know much about church, etc. I've never really gone to a church much. Well, I'll fess up. I've only been in one a couple times. Once was when we got married. Georgia wanted a church wedding. Ya know how that is."

"Yes, I know how it is...wanting a church wedding. I think it's the only way to go. But, church is so much more to me, that I have difficulty understanding being without it. What do you find as the real purpose in life?"

"Holy smokes! Ann, you sure come up with some good questions. My ole buddy, Eddie Glickmond, always has some ready answers to that. But, I don't know that I am ready to accept his ideas at this point. A, gee, I never have gotten into this kind of discussion with a lady before. We'll have to get together sometime and discuss this more in depth."

"Well, actually I'd like that. You serious about this serious discussion?"

"You bet I am. Course we'd have to do this over, say, dinner or something. Oh, I know you're in a hurry right now. Call you next week, say Monday?"

"Sure, be fine. A, Paul I think I really better be going. I am part of one of the meetings pastor Brown is attending tonight. He goes before the church council and hopefully gives them his decision as to whether he has decided to accept the call or not. It's kind of unusual to do it this way. Well, that's a long story, but anyway I want to be there. That's why I wanted to talk to him and his wife over golf. Just wanted to get to know them a little better."

"Well, what ever. Anyway I enjoyed the golf, the coffee and the conversation. I will definitely call you Monday. OK?"

"Sure, thanks again for understanding. Bye bye."

Chapter 4
Andrew's Intro

"Paul! Oh, hello I'm so glad I caught you. Paul I know I'm imposing on a new friendship, but- couldn't get anyone. I'm in trouble. Need a lift. Could you help?"

"No problem. What happened?"

"Oh nothing serious. I guess I'm making it sound worse than it is. My car won't start and I'm late for the meeting. Could you possibly give me a lift over to church? I do so want to make it."

"Hey, no problem. Glad to. Late for the meeting huh? I'll be right over. Let's see, Oak Grove area - I still have your card...."

"It's just down from the school."

"What school? Oh, Oak Grove school. Yeah, yeah – I know where it is. I can find you. Be right there."

At Ann's

"Aw, hey! Nice place. Oh yeah, you're in a hurry. Hop in."

"Paul, I really appreciate this. You don't know how important this is to me. I feel I just must be there."

"Hey, that's what friends are for. We are friends, aren't we?"

"Yes, I do consider you a friend, Paul. And I really appreciate this. Looks like I owe you again...."

"No - o problem. Hey, that church is down here, isn't it?"

"Yes, yes I'm sorry, wasn't thinking. Couple more blocks, then right at the light."

At Church

"Oh, we're seven minutes late. Paul, Thank you so much. I

really do appreciate this. You're welcome to stay if you like. But, don't worry I'm sure I can get a ride home with someone." "Couldn't leave you stranded. Sure, if it's OK, I'll stick around. Might be interesting." "Great, come on in. We're meeting in the conference room." "Hello, Ann. Glad you could make it. We're just getting started." "Bob this is a friend of mine. Gave me a lift. My car wouldn't start. Paul, meet Bob McGee. Bob, Paul Davies. I asked him to stay." "Great. Pleased meet you Paul. Have a seat."

***

"Gentlemen – and ladies – thank you for coming. I'm sure you know why we are here. We have discussed this at length for some time and now we have the privilege of hearing from one of the pastors we are considering tonight to give us some insight on his consideration of this difficult, but important matter. I think we all have aired our concerns sufficiently, so the purpose of this meeting is solely to hear from Pastor Brown and to try to understand his thoughts on the subject. So, without further ado I'll call on Pastor Brown now and he'll give you time for questions later. Pastor."

"Thank you, George, and thank you, friends, for permitting me this privilege. I know you have given me more than the usual time and consideration in this matter. I am grateful. It means to me that you are as concerned and interested as I. This certainly has been a long and tedious struggle for me. I entered this profession a little later in life than most I think and I feel I must do the most with the rest of my life that I can.

"I have considered this particular matter with great concern and prayer. And I know you have, also. I am realistic enough to know that it's wise to face facts. I know my position. I would be the first black pastor of you church. I am told even the first black person. I understand that. I understand your concern for that situation as to its reflection on my ability to communicate with your congregation. I have taken this and many other things into my consideration of this call. I have at long last made a decision. I believe I have a message and a ministry to bring to this church and to this congregation.

"I believe our work is above our physical differences, and overcoming this small difference will make us all stronger. I am firm in the decision I have made and now present to you this proposal. I would like to go before your congregation and preach a typical sermon, as I know is often done.

"By a typical sermon I mean one of the kind I would be continuing to present to this congregation and community. Not a get acquainted with me personally sermon or an attempt to please all types, but a real from the soul message.

"This, I hope will give you an insight into my mission here. I have decided. If you have not yet decided, I suggest to you this method of making the decision. Thank you."

"Thank you pastor Brown. This does help us along the way. We appreciate this information and your suggestion. Yes, an introduction type sermon is often done and I believe is certainly in order here. Are there any more questions from the floor or, should we adjourn and consider this further?"

"I think we have considered it enough already. I move we accept Pastor Brown's suggestion and schedule a Sunday ASAP."

Seconded, approved and adjourned.

"Wow Ann, I guess ole Pastor Brown kinda laid it on the line huh?"

"Yes, he is direct and I guess that's one thing I like about him and I think it's a quality we need. That's not the only reason, though. From talking to him I get a real feeling of understanding the world as it is and his wanting to minister to this – right here, right now, not something far off in the mystical distance."

"Oh yeah, what does he say, repent!?"

"That too, of course. But he sees the importance of first understanding a person, where they are now; then showing them how to move to something better, and a good reason to repent."

"Oh man, if he can do that, he's quite a genius."

"Well, he's as close to genius as anybody I know. That I respect. But really that's what Christianity is all about."

"Really, I thought it was, 'be good or you'll go to you know where'."

"It's much more than that. Based on love, actually. Maybe you should hear Pastor Brown's sermon. You might be impressed."

"Aw, yeah, I probably would...I...."

"Well Paul, tell you what. If you're serious...I'd like to help you with that. A, we could even call it a date. Since I owe you. Course...there's a catch...you have to go to church. I'll even throw in dinner. My turn. You accept?"

"Oh -a - ha - hey – sure! I wouldn't turn down a date with you. Sure it's a date."

"There is one other catch...."

"Oh no, what else?"

"I do teach a Sunday school class, as you know, before church. Can't miss. I'll either have to pick you up and let you go to Sunday school class with me, or I can meet you at church...11:00 o'clock?"

"A, Sunday school!? Hey, Ann I have never had a gal ask me for a date before and I didn't expect to be picked up. I don't know if I'm ready for Sunday school. I'll meet you at church. OK?"

"Sure, maybe just a little before 11:00 so we won't be late. OK?"

"Oh sure, sure."

"Good! See you then. Bye bye."

Sunday Morning Again

"Well, hello, merry sunshine. Who hit you with the ugly stick? You look like you bet on a long shot at the track. What gives?"

"Aw, sit down Glick. Yeah I'll have one."

"You need one. So what's happen'un now? That babe beat you at pasture pool?"

"As a matter of fact.... She and a preacher and his wife. But that isn't the problem."

"You got to be kid'n. You need another one. Cheez, let me even buy you one. Were you sober at the time? And if you were with a preacher I suppose you had to play it straight, then, huh? Anything go right?"

"Yeah, no – I mean, sure. It's something different."

"OK, OK. From the beginning, slow. I'll try to read your lips and understand how mixed up you are. Go."

"Well, you told me to go call her. I did. We played golf with the preacher and his wife. They talked about serious stuff, church and all. I didn't dig it all, but ya know, you gotta agree with some of it. Well, it seems this guy, Pastor Brown, is going to possibly be their preacher in their church – Ann's, and, well, first of all, he's black and they ain't, and – well, most of all he's a neat talker. Ann says he's got a lot on the ball, and well, Ann asked me for a date and we're go'un to church to hear him talk, an...."

"Whoa, wait a minute. It's Ann now. She asks you for a date and you're go'un to church? You met her mother yet?"

"Oh get off it, Glick, this is serious!"

"That's what I'm afraid of. Look old buddy. Last time I told you it was one of two things. Well it still is, and it's this. Dump her. Get out before you start hearing wedding bells or, well you know how you talked about Georgia and all. How there was nothing really there, just sex – not that that's bad. But you know you were look'un for something else, something real and all that stuff. Well if you're snif'un on that, hey, that's kinda scary, ya know? Be careful. - Go ahead, go to church. That ought to tell you some'thun. Hey, bring her down to your world. You say she's a golfer. Bring her down on Sunday. Let ole Glick check her over. You say she's a looker...."

"Well she has Sunday school class Sunday morning, but...."

"Sunday school!? Cheez, what next? You go'un to Sunday school, too?"

"Well, she did invite me...."

"Aw, man! This gal's a mover. Hey, look, with all this church and Sunday school stuff, and you're still interested, there must be some deep itch gett'un you. Check it out. When the long shots do come in they pay good, real good, right?"

"Yeah, you're right as usual...."

"What? You said I'm right? I changed my mind. Go get your head looked into. You're sick!"

Chapter 5
Somewhere

Those Angels Communicate Again

"Andrew and even Paul are along the way."

"Yes, they are. Andrew has come a long way, and he has responded to guidance. Now, he faces his next great challenge. He will survive, of course, but it will bring out some struggles."

"Struggles that will again strengthen."

"It is difficult sometimes to remember they are at that level and that these things often promote development. They have such a short time there actually. We have to remember, it seems long to them while going through it."

"Not only long to them, but too often the concerns of that life can seem so important that all of their energies are expended accomplishing things which are limited to that world, and afterwards when they leave it, they have nothing developed for the future."

"This is one of the hardest things to accomplish here. This world they are in does seem to them to be all there is, and it's very difficult to establish the belief that the real existence comes later and also that it is affected by the small time there."

"We have representatives there, but again so do the others and they are very clever at making use of the worldly things, making them seem all there is, and more important, often it does affect them there."

"Yes, it's difficult to see that the real life can come through, even at that time, and be so much more."

"It is easier to bring this out through struggles sometimes, as you observed, than when everything – on their earth anyway – seems to be going very well."

"We, of course, must see that the right influence is available when they seek something, or ask for help, because of some difficulty that has caused them to seek something higher."

"Andrew is seeking help now. Let us support him. He is trying to open the door to take great steps in the right direction!"

Andrew's Intro
(Sunday)

"Hi Ann. Sorry I'm late...."

"Oh, hello Paul. No, your OK. It's only 10:57. Glad you could make it. It's a really important Sunday to me. Pastor Brown's sermon and all. I want to hear what he has to say. After, well, you heard what he had to say the other night."

"Yeah. Say this is kinda big place isn't it? A, Ann, do we have to do anything – like kneel or anything?"

"No, no, just be yourself, relax and enjoy the sermon. I'll show you. We do go through the liturgy first. Then Pastor's sermon comes. Well here it is in the bulletin. See?"

The Sermon

"Good morning all. I'm very pleased to have this opportunity to come before you. As you may know I am one of the possible choices you have for a succeeding pastor here at Trinity when your present pastor moves on to his next call. I thank you for offering me this chance to speak to you today.

"I feel I have two missions here today. One is of course to bring to you a message from the word of God. This certainly is way ahead of whatever is in second place.

"Also, I feel I must convey to you a complete satisfaction that the person before you is the kind of person you can completely put your confidence in to be your spiritual leader in the coming years or not! I have thought and prayed on this long and hard. And I have made my decision. I wish to be your pastor. I think I have considered everything. I have considered and do not think it should be taken lightly that I am not only the first black pastor, but, I hear, the first black man to set foot in this church.

"I am realistic enough to know that this is of some concern. I am deeply aware of that. I am aware of it from my own point of view and I am completely satisfied that what I have to do here has nothing to do with the color of my skin, or yours. What I have to do is far more important. I hope and pray you have, or will reach the same conclusion.

"I have spent far more energy considering how I would do the work here that should be done and how I should go about it.

"As I always do, I looked to the Scriptures. My favorite book is either Matthew or Luke. I haven't made up my mind yet. But as I looked again at Matthew, I see that he ended his complete message of Jesus' ministry here by telling us, in a summation sort of way, to '-go and make disciples of all nations.'"

"Interesting to me that He said 'make disciples'. Not, spread the word or bring people to church. This means to me instilling in them a true desire to be and do all that Jesus asks us to do.

"I have found that this, strangely enough, is a hard thing to do. I would think that people would be eager to learn the secrets of life, both spiritual and physical.

"The message of Christianity is: Our God is a loving God. So loving that he stepped down from his throne in heaven and walked this dirty world with us, suffered humiliation and death just to save us and provide for us eternal life.

"What other gods that people worship have done that or would be willing to do that?

"This is the greatest message. The greatest true story there is. Why don't people accept it? I don't know. But I know they are very slow to do so. They seem to look for something else. Something more or different they can hang on to. Many need something down to earth, nitty-gritty. Why did my mommy and daddy get a divorce? Why was my son killed by a drive-by shooting when he had nothing to do with it? I searched for these answers and got a clue from a fourteen-year-old who told me, 'When all else fails - read the instructions.'

"'What instructions?' I asked.

"'The Ten Commandments', she replied.

"I thought about this a long time. I finally had to have her explain it to me. She was in my Sunday school class.

"'Well, take the sticky one,' she said, 'ole #6[2], you know, adultery. If there was no adultery we wouldn't even know what Aids is, or any of those other so called social diseases. If there was no adultery we would have no abortion problems. It's not the one half of one percent or what ever, for medical reasons that's the problem. It's the teen mother, who wants neither to raise an illegitimate child nor to have an abortion. That's the problem!

"The worst of all is the millions of illegitimate kids who are born and raised by one parent at best, who miss the family warmth and good instructions of life, and often know only the way of the street. The experts we so often hear from say 90% of the trouble causers in this world come from such a background.'

"'And another thing,' she said, 'many of the divorces are basically caused by or related to adultery.

"'Seems to me adultery is the basic cause for all our troubles. But still everyone pays no attention and seem to think it's OK. I can't understand it!'

"Then she hesitated a second or two and said, 'And safe sex

---

[1] Sometimes numbered 7

is the biggest lie of the 20th century!' Wow, talk about 'out the mouth of babes', a fourteen year old and summed it all up in that statement. Adultery, if you wanted to look at it this way, you could say the devil picked a great tool. He even has us working for him. Many of us support adultery for one reason or another or find no fault in it for one reason or another. And the Ten Commandments, we view them as some negative restrictions instead of the guide to a happier life.

"I believe it's true. I believe most of our problems today would go away as she describes if only we would follow instructions! Stop and think. If everyone or if even more people followed the Ten Commandments as we are commanded to do, what a change this world would experience!

"Love God! Keep the Sabbath. Honor father and mother. Don't kill. Don't steal. Don't commit adultery, don't lie and don't want to access what others have.

"Have we heard it before? Of course! Have we heard it many times? Of course. Do we do it? Tragically, *no!*

"Weigh the values! On one side we have the love of God, love for one another, no killing, no stealing, all the benefits of no adultery, no lying, no coveting - and that spells a truly better world. And on the other side - well, the mess of this world. And why don't we change? And it would be a change - we just don't want to. That's all.

"What do we come to worship for if we go away the same person - with the same attitude? What do we do - go home and say - wow, that was a neat service today - and let it stop there? Do we believe it? If we do, let me ask you this - eye to eye. Why do we do it? Why do we ignore the command of God through Matthew – to make disciples of all nations. Maybe we have to start with ourselves. But that's great! You want something better? You want a better life - right here right now - here it is. I challenge you to tell me why you won't do this - now! I promise you this - you *will* have a better life - you will feel better - you will even be excited. You will be accepting

God and his ways and you will enjoy it forever! All of the other things that you should do will fall into place because you are accepting God and His will.

"I love you as brothers and sisters of God's family. It hurts me when things are not going well in our family. Help me to help one another. Help me to share the secret of life, which should be no secret, and make us all live a better life - now and forever. Amen."

Angels

"Beautiful. A true basic concept, and badly needed since so much damage has already been done!"

After the Sermon

"Ah, hey, Ann that was some sermon. I think I see what you mean about Pastor Brown. But, a, you mentioned something about dinner. Let me take you, I feel better that way. I would like to talk about it; kinda got my attention. You have some stuff to do here, or sump'thun?"

"No I'm ready to depart. Paul, let me take advantage of you again and invite you to come to my place. I have a roast ready to go. We can relax and I'd love to talk. OK?"

"Some taking advantage. Ann you overwhelm me. How could a guy refuse such an invitation. Well, since we both drove, I guess I'll have to meet you there."

"Man, here I go to 'her place' for Sunday dinner !! What is this? I can't believe it's happening!?"

Ann's House

"Aw - Ann - this has got to be the best place in town to have Sunday dinner. Say, you sure have a talent for making a place look comfortable and well, homey, it's nice!"

"Oh, thanks. Make yourself at home. I'll just warm this stuff up. Won't take long. Sunday paper's on the table."

Am I dreaming - make yourself at home! Sunday paper - dinner - and she wants to talk! And that church thing. How'd she get me in there so easy? And I liked it! I mean I was interested or – I don't know what I mean. Hey, I should be scheming. Here I sit like some old married man or something. What am saying!?

After Dinner

"Well, Paul, what did you think of Pastor Brown's sermon?"

"It was very interesting. A, several things. Most of all I don't think I ever looked at the Ten Commandments that way, I guess. I just thought of them, like he says, as a, well, what did he say – a negative something. Like don't do this or you've had it. But he said, and I had to laugh, follow instructions when all else fails. I guess all else is failing."

"Interesting way to look at it. And how adultery is the basis for almost all our troubles. When you think about it, it's true."

"A, yeah, well, I can't believe it. Seems different talking adultery so openly with a lady. I know we're adults and all. A, hey, *you're* different. You know that?"

"Oh, I'm sorry...."

"No no, don't be sorry. A, Ann I don't mean it's bad; it's good! I don't usually find myself at a loss for words. But, well, you've been awfully nice and very different from most – a – anyone I ever met before and I guess I'm having a little trouble knowing just how I want to act."

"Don't act. Just be yourself."

"That's just it. If I did be myself, you'd throw me out of here. You know, come to my place, make yourself at home – you slip'un into something comfortable and all, and we're adults and, well, I don't want to be myself. Not that you're – awe I'm getting in deep and ...."

"I know Paul, I guess I did give you a come on, and I certainly didn't mean it that way. And with this Pastor Brown thing and you know him and all. I guess I don't know how to act a little myself."

"Yeah, you got me talk'un to myself here. We should know all the answers and all the questions. But seems like some new ones are coming up for me, and I don't know how to express it. Hey, your nice people Ann, and I like being with you and I don't want to blow it. A, don't take that the wrong way. You know, we really haven't spent much time together and I guess I really don't know you, but yet I feel like I do, or want to. Awe, I feel like a schoolboy rattling on. You've been pretty nice to a guy who ran into your car, for starters...."

"Oh, what's after starters?"

"Well, for guy who thinks he's been around the block, I sure am running into some new territory. A couple of new territories. For seconders – about this church thing. I know I am not a church person, but, well, I thought it was like, 'go to church and be good etc. - or go to hell'. And there's these rules that God wants us to follow and if you don't, too bad."

"Well, yes Paul, there is such a thing as the judgment. And it's, of course, nothing to be taken lightly. But what Pastor Brown is saying is that God's whole plan is based on love. Salvation is based on love. And His commandments are for us, not Him. He's not worried about being hit by some drive-by shooter or what to do with an illegitimate child. But out of love He does not want us to have these problems. So He gives us these instructions. And He expects us to follow them so we don't cause trouble for ourselves or others. And, as Pastor Brown says, it gives us a better life now, and always!"

"Awe, man, that's all pretty heavy, but if what you say is true, why haven't people been jump'un on this long time ago?"

"I really don't know. Again, - it's like Pastor said. - It's everything to gain and nothing to lose. And for me, that's why I do all this. It's everything."

"I don't know what to say. I guess I keep saying that. This – a – is sort of mind boggling. I think I have to let it all sink in a little. A, I always thought I was a quick to catch on guy. Don't have to draw me a picture, you know? I, well I just have to think about it."

"You said a couple of things were new. What else?"

"Awe, you asked – kinda brings me back to that other thing. I am in new territory. I'm on the defensive. Not really – here I go again – I mean, what I really mean is it's important. And again Ann, I enjoy being with you very much. It's a good thing, even from the first – the dumb car thing and all. I know it's been short and.... Well, being with you is different. That's a tired old line, right? Funny how when you want to be sincere about something you've heard said thousand times, but somehow you want to make it real this time, you don't know how to do it. Ann, I really do like being with you, and I want to see you and be with you more. Do you mind?

"No, Paul I don't mind and it's nice to hear what you said. I've thought about it too, being brief and all. But, oh, no! The phone!"

"Let it answer itself."

"I would but I'm anxious to hear what people are going to say about Pastor's sermon."

***

"Hello. Yes, yes this is Ann. Oh, hi Ed. Yes I was. Oh, OK, later tonight? Yes I'll be there. OK, bye bye."

"Well, that was Ed from church, you know. He says they are going to meet tonight to discuss the outcome of the appearance of Pastor Brown. Evidently there's some feeling both ways."

Church Council Meeting

"Well, we did it! In spite of better judgment we let him take the pulpit. And, he did it. He couldn't have picked a more touchy subject – adultery. You saw Evensons walk out! We've tried to control such outbursts in this church for years, and now we let a black man splatter it all over."

"Afro-American."

"You know what I mean. We won't have ten people in the church next Sunday."

"Ah I don't know that I completely agree with you George. I think that's exactly what we need. I think that's what's ailing our church right now. We've been, what does the Book say, like - lukewarm and spewing us out of His mouth."

"Don't go trying to quote scriptures to me. You know how things are. Get real! That's going to be the last nail in the coffin. That'll sink this church, and I don't want to be a party to it. We've done too much damage already."

"Well, George I have to say it, I can't agree with you, either. I think that's the greatest sermon I've heard in the twelve years we've been coming here. I think in the past we've been afraid to speak, but I'm going to stick my neck out and move that we accept Pastor Andrew Brown as our next pastor here at Trinity."

"Oh fine!"

"We have a motion on the floor, and second, thank you. That brings us to 'discussion' officially. Do I hear any more discussion?"

"I just discussed it. And I can't see how you could accept a motion to make this – this pastor a part of our church."

"I agree with the motion. I can't see how we can claim to be Christian and let a racial or color concern interfere with our work here at Trinity. As for his message, well I think it was right on. If we don't get the Bible view of these things in church, where are we going to get them. Especially our young people. The media certainly holds nothing back, and neither does the Bible. Where do we get off holding back on teaching our kids what the real truth is? Talk about the sin of doing nothing. We've been presented with a real message and a man who wants to pursue it. I think we would be negligent if we didn't support him. I vote 'aye.'"

"I agree and I call for the question."

"Any more discussion?"

"Question."

"The question has been called for. We'll take a secret ballot. Simply write yes or no on your slips and pass them in."

"Nine for - two against. Motion passed."

Chapter 6
They Communicate Again

"The first steps for Andrew have been taken. He is attempting to reach people there by showing them that the way is meaningful and beneficial in their world as in the real world."

"I think he is aware that it must be pointed out that the real message, love, in their word is above their world but also exists in their world."

"It seems they are so worldly centered, of their world that is, that they do not relate to the real existence beyond it. Andrew is trying to bring them to understand the benefits of both."

"He must be careful not to limit his teachings to the values of the world they live in."

"Of course. Although they are surely there, the greater existence is of infinitely more importance."

Andrew and Chucks

"What's the matter, young man? You look like you're bear'un the troubles of the world."

"Young man, Ha! I feel a 150. Am, I did it again. Who did I think I was, gett'un up before an all white church – me a black man – an' tell'en 'em 'don't commit adultery'. A stranger in their church, and supposed to make a good impression. They probably think it's us, the black folks who need to hear about adultery. I should've remembered the instruction from my seminary professor, like, don't get too heavy, especially at first. Wait until you know your congregation or you'll lose them before you start. Oh, Am I did it again, me and my big mouth.

I've come so far! Will I ever learn? I had a tough time with this decision. It's a big church, a big chance and all. I thought it was my ego at work. But I thought about it long and hard. After all I want to do and accomplish as much as I can.. So, I decided this was the thing to do. And now I've blown it!"

"Honey, you're be'un too tough on yourself. You know what you felt when you told me years ago you had to do this thing, and how you felt your life was not what you wanted, and you had to say what you had to say – no matter what! Don't forget that. Nobody said it was going to be easy. You're trying to do the good work. That comes with some sacrifice. You told me that. It's easy to do the easy things."

"Aw, baby, your right, you're always right. It's just that my insides are coming apart. I feel like I made a fool of myself and worse. I blew it. I blew my first big chance."

(Little Later)

"Feeling better? No? Well maybe you ought to consult a little higher authority. You know you felt right when you did it and that's the real way you want it – is it not?"

"Right again baby. Maybe it's one of those things that will bear its fruit later, or maybe I just learned a good lesson."

Georges Place

"That you George? Well, what's eat'un on you? You don't have to slam things."

"I tell you there's just no understanding some people. All the work and effort we put into this church, trying to save it, and these people want to put a big talking black man in the pulpit. I don't know."

"What are you upset about, George?"

"What am I upset about!? I just told you! They want that guy to be our new pastor. That's what. I can't understand it."

150

"Well, George maybe it's not as bad as you think. I was talking to the girls down at Mary's...."

"Oh no, don't tell me he's con'd the women, too. Handsome black guy and all – give'em a chance. I can just hear it."

"Now just a minute George there's some things here that make sense. First of all, his being black has nothing to do with it and you might as well face it and forget it. But, what he says does. You know people have been talking for years that something needs to be done. The things that have been going on, well, all over, are just too much and now we're feeling it right here. Mary Ann was saying she wants her daughters to go to a private school, but they can't afford it. Angela says her second-grader comes home with language you wouldn't believe and her older sister is pregnant! Fifteen years old and she's pregnant! You hear that! And you want to get on your hi horse about what this man says in the pulpit. Well I think he's right on."

"Oh right on. They got you talking that way already. You women'll go for anything that's in. Do I have to listen to this in my own house? I'm going to The Den."

The Den

"Hey George! Put it in the cushion and have a cup."

"I think I need more than a cup."

"Oh well, have a saucer!"

"Please, spare me. I've had enough. First the council, then I hear it at home. Now I have to listen to your punk humor."

"You don't have to listen."

"Yeah, I guess. I've heard enough already. Tell me something good."

"Well I hear we're going to have a new preacher."

"Oh no! That I don't want to hear. Let's not joke about it."

"Wasn't joking. Matter of fact, I think it's just what we need."

"And how do you justify that remark?"

"Hey, you are upset aren't cha? Well you know, you can't deny this society of ours is in a mess. Everybody's talked about it. And we don't know where to start to fix it. There ain't enough policemen nor programs nor nothun else that'll really matter. I think the only way is the old Vince Lombardi thing: 'back to basics.' And that's what he's talk'un about."

"Who's talking about?"

"The new preacher. Jeez, listen up. You know what I mean!"

"OH, the new preacher, huh? You talk like it 's all settled."

"Well, might as well be, George. It's all over town."

Church
(Later)

"Oh, hi Ed, George, Mrs. Duncan, Paul!! Well, am I glad to see you!? I didn't know you were coming...."

"Well, you didn't invite me. I had to find out for myself. Thanks a lot."

"Oh Paul. I'm sorry. I...."

"Just kidd'un, just kidd'un no problem. All hands meeting, huh? I read about it in that handout thing I got last Sunday."

"Yes, it was in the bulletin. Well I'm glad you're here. Big day. We decide about our choice of pastors. That is, so far it's Pastor Brown or not."

"Yeah, I know. What do we do, vote?"

"Yes, it's an all member vote. The council has made their recommendation. Now it has to be approved by the congregation. You do have to be a member to vote."

"You mean I can't vote. I was going to bring some friends in...."

"Sorry, you do have to be a member."

"You can't campaign for the one you want?"

"Well, in a way. It's true only members can vote, but there

has been a lot of talk going around. I couldn't believe it and it was among people who don't even belong to Trinity."

"Yeah, I guess."

Mr. and Mrs. Geo Duncan's Pew

"Wow, you know the church is almost full!?"

"Huh, we won't have any trouble getting a quorum."

"Well, they're going to get right to it. Secret ballot of course."

"Sure, what else?

***

"Here comes the count. It's what!? It's unanimous!? I don't believe it - with this many? And all I've heard! George, unanimous?"

OK, OK, so I changed my mind. Can't I change my mind? I mean after you and the council and all the guys at The Den and all I've heard all week. I even heard people wrote letters and the church got phone calls. Well what was I going to do, be a jerk about it?"

"No, George, no. Don't be a jerk."

Outside

"Surprised? A land slide, huh?"

"Really. I knew he was getting a lot of support, but to get everyone's vote. It's truly unbelievable. I don't know what to think about it."

"I thought you guys called these things miracles, don't cha?"

"Yes, Paul, I suppose we do."

Angels

"If they only knew!"

"Well Ok, hey, you don't have to cry about it. Aw, hey, I'm sorry Ann. I didn't mean to make light of it. I'm sorry. Really."
"You don't have to apologize. It's just that I feel so good and it's a relief. I'm OK."
"Good! Say, speaking of miracles, what does it take to get you alone for a while? Would dinner in the next state do it?"
"Oh, yes, Paul, that would be great. It would be nice to relax and get away from it for a while. Next state? You serious?"
"Well there is a place down the road a ways, by the river, individual booths, kinda cozy."
"Sounds nice. Do they serve seafood?"
"As matter of fact...."

Chuck's Place - By the River

"Ou ou, this *is* nice."
"Hoped you'd like it. It's old-fashioned – low ceiling, jukebox, booths, and even a dance floor. You relate to jukebox and dance floor?"
"Paul, you devil, you've been reading my diary. I love to dance and I haven't seen a jukebox like that in years."
"Great, but don't tell me you haven't danced in years."
"As a matter of fact, but one thing at a time. About that seafood, I'm starved."
"Hey, they've got a combo here that'll take care o'that. Crab, shrimp, chowder, let me recommend it. May I order for you Mrs. Winfield, and make a wine selection?"
"Please do. Sounds great."
"Um-m, Paul that was super delicious. And this place – something about it makes you feel sort of relaxed, homey I guess. Makes you want to take your shoes off or something."
"Neat to see we have some things in common, seafood. You like this place. A, you ever dance with you shoes off?"
"Paul, you *have* been reading my diary. On Sunday afternoon?"

"So what? You did say you liked to dance."

"Must be the wine. Love to!"

Um - I've danced with some babes before - but, man what is it. She just fits. And dance - she floats. Got a lotta woman here. Did they put something in that wine. Cloud-ninesville!

"A, Ann you dance...."

"Sh - h - ish, just dance."

Aw man - when she said that and then pulled up a little closer.... Have I been live'un in a small world or what? I never felt like this before. Excited isn't the word. Man I feel good all over. Good isn't even the word. It's like they say - you can't describe it - you have to experience it!

"Um - m- m-"

"Play it again?"

"Let's sit down a minute."

"OK."

"You know, Paul you took me to dreamland there for minute. That song, the dance, and all. You're dangerous."

"Wow, well I hope so. Was it a good dreamland?"

"Sure was. That song stirred up some memories and I told you I love to dance. What dance school did you go to...."

"Ha, glad you liked the show. We can get a rerun for a quarter you know."

"I know. I'm still soaking up the last one. Who told you to take me to a place like this, feed me seafood and then dance like that. That's illegal warfare. You're taking advantage of a poor girl, you know that?"

"No, I didn't, but there's a bit going on, on both sides. I kinda visited a little dreamland myself...."

"Really?"

"Yeah, really Mrs. Winfield. I never believed in chemistry and all that stuff but there's something happening. I keep asking myself, am I falling for you, and I keep telling myself, 'yes.' And that was even before all of the seafood and the wine."

Um - the look she's giv'un me - you can't describe - but I love it!

Another Dance

"You, Ann you, did you ever kiss a guy on the dance floor on Sunday afternoon?"
"Not yet."

Chapter 7
Class Experiences

Sunday AM

"Hello, Glick? Hey, this is Paul. Listen I won't be play'un today OK? No, I'm just fine. I just got another thing going. Yeah, I know it's Sunday. But I...hey...will ya listen....I'm busy. Go buy yourself one. You're lucky - you won't lose any money on the green today. Yeah. Ann's fine. Yeah, OK nosy...so it's Ann again...so I'm see'un her a lot...OK so it's been weeks, all right month, so it's been months. None of your stink'un business, OK? No, *we're* not play'un golf - - oh, my heart bleeds. Look, go take your ole lady golf'un. No, don't, she'd probably beat cha. Hey, later. Yeah, yeah, ga bye."

Sometimes I wonder why I put up with that turkey - he drives me nuts - yet I don't know - who else? Maybe we deserve each other. I guess I've sorta leaned on him in a couple a tough times. But I've got a different mission today. Seafood and dancing I can handle, but church and Sunday school!? Jeez! Man, the hook must be in deeper than I think. Maybe I better go look in the mirror. I might be sick and don't know it. Funny, if I'm sick , I never felt so good.

Church

"We go sing?"
"Yes, we all sing together first, then to class. Hang in there...you'll survive."
"You sure?"

"Sure. Look, we sit with the class first. Over there."

"There? With those? Hey, there's some lookers there. That's a Sunday school class? Where are the kids?"

"High school."

"Don't any boys go to Sunday school?"

"Yeah, we have a couple. They're not here right now. Hey, guys, this is my friend Paul. Scoot over."

Aw - man I didn't bargain for this. This is a Sunday school class? I'm glad Glick can't see me now. Look at these babes. Ya sure this is a Sunday school class?"

Class

"Well, did you finish reading Job. I guess I should bring you up to date for those who weren't here before. We started studying Job. We learned how God and the Devil made a deal to test him. He knew nothing about it, of course. Bad things happened to him. His friends came and tried to understand why these things happened to such a good man. They talked about everything they could think of, but couldn't justify it. Now, what happened in the end?"

"God told Job that there was no way he could understand these things, since he was not around in the beginning nor could he understand the ways of God's kingdom, but that he should trust God."

"Yes, good. That's a good summation. If we apply this lesson to our lives, it doesn't mean we can expect God and the Devil to be planning a test such as this for each one of us. But the point is, we don't know all that exists in God's plan and the way things work in His world. With our limited knowledge it's impossible to understand it all. Therefore, God asks us to trust in Him. Remember when we studied about eternity, how vast and unending it is in all directions. Well, these considerations enter in our attempted understanding of the things that happen to us in this life. The lesson from Job is far more important than the fact that he lost his possessions, was sick, etc. We can see that in the fact that the lesson learned is still with us today, many years later, and we still benefit from it, even though Job is long since dead and over his problems which seemed terrible at the time. It's a way of reminding us that sometimes the wisdom gained from an experience lasts long after the experience and is of much more importance. Although it is difficult for us to understand and to accept when it happens, just maybe the lesson learned far exceeds the importance or even the difficulty we go through at the time."

After Class - Ann's House

"Gee, Ann I guess I had a different idea about Sunday school. I just thought about little kids and stuff. You know, singing 'Jesus loves Me.' But, man, you guys get into some heavy stuff."

"That's what it's all about. They want to study and talk about what's happening today. Several months ago one of the girl's mother passed away. Jill, the little one on the end. They were divorced. Her father won't take her. She has to live with an uncle. Not good. So, we have been trying to study: Why bad things happen to good people."

"Come up with any good answers?"

"That *is* a tough question. But, yes I think so. The study of Job helps."

"Oh?"

"Well, you have to get into the whole thing and see the big picture. And have the faith to accept it."

"How do I get that?"

"Sometimes it's a long slow process. Involves several things usually, study for one, sometimes experience. Throw in a little prayer. Want to take the course?"

"Who's teach'un?"

"Well, if there's any seafood involved, I might take the job."

159

"OK, you're on."

"Oh, Paul, Nina's here! I wonder if something's wrong. Come on in!"

"Nina! Surprise. What are you doing here?"

"Oh, Mom, I need a little mother-daughter – you know?"

"Sure, sure honey. What's wrong?"

"Long story – Neil."

"OK, by the way, this is Paul, Paul Davies. Paul and I are good friends. Sit down. I'll get you a mocha or something. Want one, Paul?"

"Sure."

"Paul Davies?"

"Right. I haven't actually known your mother all that long, but I think she's nice people. Hey, if you and your mom want to talk, a, I'll catch you another time, OK?"

"Oh, I don't care if you don't. If you can put up with a little mother-daughter talk, it doesn't bother me and I don't think Mom will care either."

"OK, nothing bad, I hope."

"Not bad I guess. Basically, I've been going with Neil for about a year and he's asked me to marry him. Several times in fact, and, well, I'm not sure."

"If your not sure then it's easy. The answer is 'no'; 'cuse me for being blunt, but it's true. I was married, long time – divorced – bad scene. It wasn't right from the beginning. Learned a lot the hard way. The hard way's the hard way. But, I learned what I missed was the real thing, not sex, not money, not anything but the real thing. And if you have that, it'll work. If you don't it won't. That simple. Where I am now is, if there's any doubt, then the answer is 'no'. I won't do it again until I can't stand to be any other way. Until it's that way, it's 'no'!"

"Well, here you are, not Johnny Barista's best, but it's drinkable."

"Um, yeah, it's good. Ah, feel better. Thanks Mom. Really good to meet you Paul. Thanks for the good words. I guess I really should get back. Got a ton of work to do. Go'un to walk me to the car, Mom?"

"What!? Am I going to walk you to the car? You just got here! Gee, Nina. Come back when you can't stay so long.!"

"Oh, I know it's crazy but what can I say?"

"I don't know! But I'd like to hear something."

"Come on!---"

***

"Ah, I'm back. And you Mr. Davies, explain! Who's buying who seafood here? What magic spell did you cast over my daughter? I think I better check you out. Well, what?"

"I donno - she just said she was thinking of marrying Neil and I said, think it over!"

"That's it! That's all? She drives all the way over here to have a heavy talk with me and you clear it all up while I make espresso. Come on Mr. Davies, give!"

"Well, she just said, she and this Neil have been going together a year and he asked her the big question and she wasn't sure. So I said then the answer is 'no'."

"Oh, just like that?"

"Well, I explained. I said I've been through it and had to learn the hard way. If you have the real thing it will work. If you don't, it won't. If your in doubt, you haven't got it, and so the answer is 'no'."

"I can't believe it! I've spent weekends talking to her and you, you... OK, what do I owe you? Besides a great big thank you, Paul, really."

"Oh you're welcome, but your not get'un off with a lousy seafood dinner. But I'll take it. Maybe we can get into a discussion about one of those real things, if you're into 'real things.'"

"Maybe, which real things did you have in mind?"

"Several, well at least two. Anyway these two are eat'un on me the most. A, Ann I guess number one is you. I mean our relationship – a, sounds like a tired word, doesn't exactly fit. I feel it's something more - special. Been short - maybe - sorta interrupted - I guess. But I, well, I think with all my worldly wisdom etc. etc., I should be able to say something to you that is just so magnanimous that it's never been heard before. So wonderful it would just sweep you off to – I don't know where. Somewhere great. But I just keep wanting to blurt out, 'I LOVE YOU, I LOVE YOU' and it's because I do. And that's because I've got the real thing! You know about the real thing?"

"Yes, Paul I do, and I have the same feelings."

"You, you *do!* You're not kidd'un me. You really do?"

"Oh, a- um, Paul, I - I - I... you devil! Who taught you to kiss like that?"

"Oh some sexy women I've kissed all over the world. Where'd you learn?"

"Just comes naturally, if you have the real thing of course. Oh, Paul, you do have a way of netting things out and, you know, you're right. If you really love someone, nothing else matters, does it?"

"Not if you really love 'em."

"How'd you get this valuable information?"

"Well, I guess that part, I lived it! When you get it that way you get it good!"

"True. Well, what else do you know, oh, man of wisdom?"

"I know every guy who's stuck on a gal says they're really in love, it's true love etc., etc. I know that, but, well, is it experience or what? Ann, I never felt like this before! I - I... it's just so good. I'm on a high just being with you. A ... different kind of high... You know how much feeling there can be in those so called – three little words?"

"Um, are you telling me you're sure this is the real thing, Paul Davies?"

"Yes, Ann Winfield, I definitely am telling you. I love you and I believe it's the real thing. And since we're being so formal, how do you, Mrs. Winfield, attorney at law, respond to that?"

"Ha! I'd rather not think on legal terms right now. But, Ann Winfield loves you very much."

"How about one of those famous 'real thing' kisses?"

"Um-m-m-mmmmm!"

"I thought I was enlisting in your class in faith, but this will do for right now."

"Maybe later."

"Yeah, later."

Angels Again

"Sometimes things happen in strange ways, even on earth. Paul has lived most of his life on the surface. Seeing things for their face value only. And, believing he has it all figured out. But, the effect of love has brought out the deeper side of Paul. A side he didn't even know he had himself, even though it was there. He is changing, more than he knows. It is for the best!"

Paul's House

"Well, hello, Glickmond. Miss me so much you had to come pay me a visit?"

"Oh sure! Mind if I come in? It OK if I have a seat? Nice to see you, too."

"OK, OK, sit down....I'll be right there. I'll mix you one. Turn on the tube....I'll be right there."

"Don't mind if I do. Hey you don't look much different. You did go to church and all, didn't you?"

"Yeah, I want to church, cool it. It ain't all that – what you think it is. And maybe your not looking close. I think I have changed a bit. That church bit and all it's... a... well... Hey, what did ya do, come over here for a report into my private life? What did you do yourself? You go to church?"

"No, I didn't. As a matter of report. I got laced on the course. Wanda beat me!"

"Jeez, you're kidd'un. I get waxed by the preacher and his wife and your ole lady beats you. Hey, pal what are we, bottom of the totem pole?"

"I donno. You said friend Ann beat you too. Speaking of Ann...."

"Hey, cool it. Just never mind about her, OK?"

"Oh, over that soon, huh? What happened Paully, baby....She show you the door?"

"Knock it off. No she didn't. And just don't go with your wise Glickenhymer remarks, OK? Is that what you came over here for?"

"Sorry, sorry! Well, at least you don't have to get a lawyer... OOPS, I guess that's a bad word."

"Look Glick, you're on the wrong channel. Ann and I are OK. I mean really. I just didn't want to hear any of the usual Glickmond drivel, OK? It's not like that. I told you before. She's class, and not only that, I... look Eddie, I love her OK? I mean, really, for real, no games, OK?"

Aw, man, I know I'm not much at play'un the straight scene, but after all the crying in the beer we had together over the last one. And after all you told me later, I gotta wonder. You got a winner this time? A... you... a... said love. I mean, really! Not sex, nor she's upstairs or... you mean love."

"Yeah, love, real l-o-v-e love."

"Got it. Love. Real love. Well, buddy, speaking of the dead and should be forgotten past. I do remember some rather long beer conferences about how you have to learn the hard way, and how that makes such an impression on you that you couldn't get it any other way and it makes you see the way clear etc. etc. etc. Are you see'un the way?"

"Yeah, I really am. When I think about Ann and then think about all the crap I went through before. A... ya know I feel like I would have missed a..a. I don't know, the real life Glick!"

"Yeah, I got a glimmer. I saw something with Wanda. All those Sundays she's been sitt'un at home. And then she said 'If you really want to play Eddie, I'll play with you'. Course she didn't have to beat me, but I kinda got a message, ya know?"

"Yeah, I know. Comes to some people slow, huh?"

Chapter 8
Somewhere

"I see things have moved along for our Ann and her friend, Paul. It's good she is helping him. We can hope that Paul's understanding of some of the true things in his physical life will carry over to the real life. That's a bigger step and so, more difficult."

"And Paul is one of those who thinks he is greatly experienced. But, again it is of that world and he will have some difficulty seeing a completely different approach to life."

"Yes, unfortunately many never learn the simple truths and are carried away by the distractions of their life there. But it is true. They must find it, recognize it, and accept it for themselves. With all the guidance they are given, it seems strange so many do not receive it, but I remember that it is difficult to see at that level. And yet so simple."

Back to Ann's House

"Pastor! Amy! Well, what a pleasant surprise! Come in. Come in. I didn't expect to see you until the first. Are you here to stay?"

"Well, yes we are, rather unexpectedly I'm afraid. We had a little surprise where we were, in the apartment. They had a fire. Everyone had to move out. We didn't lose anything, thank goodness. But some did. And there was a lot of damage to the building. So, they asked everyone to move out. Since we had to come here sooner on later, we just came now."

"Oh, that's terrible. But, you OK? Where are you staying? When did this happen?"

"Yesterday. Yes, we're OK. They let us put our big things in storage. We haven't found a place yet...."

"Oh, Pastor, Amy, stay here. I have this big place all to myself. And I'd love the company. Please, I'd love to have you."

"Ann, Ann! We didn't come to move in; we just wanted to let you and the church know where we are and what happened etc."

"I know and I'll take care of that. But, really I want you to stay. You wouldn't turn down an old friend and golf partner, would you? Really, Amy you tell him, yes."

"Well, Ann we don't want to intrude. Maybe for the night. Until we can get settled."

"Great, but don't worry about it. I meant it when I said I'd love to have you. Don't go paying for a motel somewhere. If you leave me for an apartment or motel, I'll be insulted. You have things with you?"

"Just a few. I guess we're living out of a suitcase for now. Sometimes it's fun, but not for very long."

"I know. Come on, Amy, let me show you your room. Might need a little tidy up, but can't be too bad. Pastor, if you want to bring in your things, come on up."

"Thank you Ann. This is very nice of you and we appreciate it very much. Thank you again."

***

"You have a very nice place here, Ann, and the room is lovely!"

"Glad you like it. You make yourselves at home. Amy, if you have laundry or anything, please feel free. Washer and dryer are downstairs. In the meantime, how about a cup of coffee? Relax and tell me what's new, besides the fire."

"Well, not much with us, except the fire. We're looking forward to coming here and getting into the church work as soon as possible."

"Oh, Pastor, in here. Come have a cup."

"Thank you, Ann, and thank you again for taking us in on short notice. We were sort of out in the cold, I guess. The fire happened so quickly. I guess you don't get any advance notice on those things. Then they said everyone had to move out or stay out. We were already out. Later we just packed our bags, they let us do that, and said they'd take care of what ever was left. They weren't sure if it was safe to go back in. Smoke was everywhere. Well, anyway let's talk about something more pleasant. What's happening with you? And your friend Paul?"

"Oh, nothing real exciting with me, working for a living. Paul and I still see each other."

"Just a friend?"

"Ha! Well, Pastor you ask the best questions. Must be confession time. I do like Paul quite a lot. We seem to have some of those right vibrations. Not looking in jewelry store windows yet, but well, don't tell Paul I said that."

"Sounds great. I promise. But if you ever need any professional services, I'd be glad to help you out and very pleased by the way."

"Oh, thank you Pastor. If anything develops I'll be sure to let you know."

"OK, great. ha... ah, hope you do."

"You know, as long as I've gotten into this now. My daughter was here the other day, and she's been going with a nice guy for over a year, and he's popped the question. But, we've, well Paul and I actually have told her basically to wait. Paul told her, if in doubt, the answer is 'no'. And I guess I am getting into confession time. Anyway, I'm wondering what my daughter would say if I'm serious about a guy I've known less, in time, anyway, than she has known Neil. Sounds like a double standard, or no fool like an old fool."

"I hear you Ann, and yes you're in a 'handle it very carefully' situation. You're an adult person. I don't have to tell you there's only one way. Find true love, be sure it's real, and

169

then act on it. And live with it forever! Sounds a bit heavy, but it does happen and it does work! Have to be sure! Time usually is the best or at least one of the best testers and you're usually wise to use it. But still there's such a thing as knowing it just because you know. Recognizing it is a risky business and therefore most important, again, to be sure! I can see your daughter saying to you, 'how can you tell me one thing and you do another'. You stand in the position of possibly making a mistake with your life, and Paul's, and also setting a wrong example for your daughter. Use a little time and ask for some help from 'upstairs,' you know. It works."

"Yes, I believe that."

Angels

"Our Ann here has gotten into some earthly struggles."

"She is aware of that exposure. But she is still of this life and can see through it."

"Sometimes it is difficult to see that the two existences are definitely separate but do have some connections."

***

Pastor continues.

"The most important decisions in life are usually also the most difficult. I know. Am and I tied the knot after a short time together and at a tough time. I had just quit my job! And I was in the middle of trying to make the biggest decision of my life, entering the seminary – finally. But somehow the pull was just too strong. I couldn't do anything else, and Am helped me, quite at bit actually, with that decision and everything else since."

"Um, yes, I know those things. I guess it's knowing how to apply them to our own life and doing it that's tough. Easier to tell someone else – like you daughter."

"Yes, I think that's true, and it's one of life's repeaters.

Happens all the time. Do as I say and not as I do. It's tough. And the answer is to be sure you do the right thing, which is easy to say. But I think we have to use all the wisdom tools we have, and that includes God's instructions for us. And the more we look into that the more we realize there's more there that applies to our lives than we at first think. As you know I had to let it all out on my favorite subject from the pulpit. But it is the way and will work – and better than all the other systems one can put in place. Oh man! I'm sorry. I didn't mean to start right out preaching at you. Maybe I better light'un up a little. How's your golf game?"

"Well, if I could handle life as easily as I can my golf game and improve on it as easily, I'd have it made."

"Oh, you can improve your game that easily? You should go into the business."

"I'm bragging, but anyway I have trouble shaping my life. And the mistakes are more costly...."

"Ha! That might make a good sermon theme."

Chapter 9
Paul's Proposal

"276-7676 ----- Hi babe - hey it's been two days!"

"I know. Where you been? My phone's working."

"Ow! A gottcha! One for Ann. Well, the best I can do is make up for lost ages. How about one of those faith lessons or anything? We could take up where we left off, or hey, did I hear voices in the background? I'd be jealous, but it does sound familiar. Pastor Brown?"

"Yes, he and Amy are staying here temporarily. They had a fire in their apartment and had to move out. So they're going to stay here for a while."

"Great. Tell'um hello for me and I am sorry about the fire. Everybody OK?"

"Will do and everybody's OK. Now listen, Mr. Davies, I'm getting a bit tired of asking you out, but Pastor and Amy wanted to have some people from church come over and discuss some things. I told them to be my guest. So, listen, you turkey, you're taking me to Chuck's, OK? So when are you picking me up?"

"Well, I might try to work you in about 7:29, if nothing else comes up. And you'll be ready on time."

"That'll do. Anything else you want to tell me?"

"I love you."

"That'll do too. Goes double. Bye bye"

Chuck's

"Well, so you only go with me for my faith lessons, huh? What is it that bothers you?"

"You bother me a bunch. Aw, how can I get serious? You know how I'm have'un trouble with that church stuff and all. What would you tell someone who just doesn't understand about God and all that stuff you do?"

"I think if it was someone in my class I would probably use a different approach, but for you my opening remarks would be a bit more personal. It's really hard to know where to start. But when I think of what I believe in, I compare it with how I consider someone I am very fond of – my daughter or you, for instance. I get a similar good feeling. I think of you more deeply and real than other people. I want to be with you, do what you do, feel and enjoy what you do. I want to live and enjoy life with you. It's the same real feeling I get with God. I found out that his ways are best. Not only that, but He loves me – enough to die for me. It's true love Paul. It's the <u>real,</u> real thing."

"Wow, Ann! Wait a minute. You're something else, you know. Not only do you ask me out, you give me a real lesson in life and then tell me you want to enjoy life with me. Hey, babe I'm supposed to be telling you *that*! Honey, babe, you overwhelm me! You got my head spin'un. All I can say is 'it's true, it's true.' I mean I love you too...."

"Sorry, guess I just had to blurt out a few things too. Too big to hold back. You asked."

"Yeah, I did. And I like what I heard. I guess I have to go back to what I said about me using some of the same old phrases. They may be old and have been said before, but sure carry a new meaning right now. You know all the meaning that's in 'I love you' – *now*?"

"I sure do and it goes for both things we're talking about - it's real!"

Medium Long Silence and Some Long Looks

"Ann you've got me go'un in two directions. One, well,

kinda new to me. Up to now I thought my answer to just about everything was - 'Been there – done that,' but you, you lawyer you, you've opened up a lot of new facts in the case. I need some more time to consider the evidence. But let's get back to this other thing. Sweetheart – honey – babe - do you realize you said you wanted to live your life with me? You know I have a tape recorder under my coat. I'm going to hold you to that!"

"You know what? I don't mind if you do?"

Ann's House - Again

"Oh, hello, Ann, you're back. And Paul, nice to see you."

"Hello Pastor, nice to see you too. Say, sorry to hear about the fire. Everything OK?"

"Yes, we're OK. Nothing of ours damaged. Inconvenience mostly for us. And for Ann – having to put up with us."

"Hey, I think it's good you're here. You can keep an eye on her for me. She's quite a mover, ya know."

"Yes, she is. But usually moves in the right directions, I think?"

"You got that right. But I tell ya what? I'm interested in moving her in one direction right now and you can help me."

"All right, fine. What can I do for you Paul?"

"First, this calls for a little get-together. Mrs. Brown available? I'll get Ann in here."

***

"Well, now that we're here together – thank you. I want to make this as legal and binding as possible. You see, it's important. So I wanted to have some witnesses. Even one representing the Church and all... Ann, hold my hand. Ann Winfield, in the presence of God and these witnesses, I ask you, will you marry me and love me the rest of my life? If so, answer, 'I will.'"

"Paul, Paul! I will - I will - you...you...."
"Um, you don't have to cry about it. I believe you."
"Paul, you may kiss the bride to be."

Another One of Those Kisses

"Well, Paul, with the possible exception of one other, that's the greatest proposal I've ever taken part in. Congratulations! And best wishes to you both!"

"Yes, God''s blessings on both on you and may you have a long, happy married life."

"Thank you. - - - - - - -Paul - Paul...."

"Well, Ann, I didn't know part of a preacher's function was to witness proposals, but it sure was a pleasure.

Chapter 10
Ann Davies - Ann's Party

Later

"You know, Ann, you sure do things to me. I'm actually looking forward to being with you in your Sunday school class today. Boy, ole Glickmond would flip if he heard me say that."

"Well, I'm glad Paul. You know one of the girls actually asked me about you. Must be that tall, dark, handsome appearance of – no that couldn't be. Well I don't know, maybe I don't want you going to my class."

"That so? Well, you're stuck with me now. Maybe that'll teach you not to take me for granted."

"Get in there!"

Good morning, girls. Oops, I'm sorry. Too used to having all girls. Welcome a ...."

"Mrs. Winfield, this is John and he's deaf. Marion is going to sign for him, if you don't go too fast."

"I'll try not to. Marion, tell John 'welcome' and we're glad to have him in the class. And if he has a question just raise his hand. OK?"

"Sure."

"I didn't know you could sign, Marion. Where'd you learn?"

"Actually both Mary Ellen and I do. We started last year when John fell and had his accident. Remember, we were talking about helping people and all. John's Mary Ellen's cousin."

"Oh, you didn't tell me. That's great."

"We didn't know how it would work out at first. John was

down and he didn't want us around, and, well, that's why."

"Well, looks like it's working out very well. Gee, girls, I think that's great that you are doing this. And now John is here."

"There is a reason, sort of. A... we told John about how things happen sometimes and everything, and how, well, you know, how the real important things are eternal and all. Oh, I don't know, I can't explain it. But – well, anyway, John has problems with accepting it all – God, eternity and everything, you know."

"I see. Sometimes we all do. We'll try to cover some of that as we go along. Remember the answer to things like this are not simple one-word answers. They take understanding from knowledge and study, both from scripture and from life and also help from God Himself.

"The first thing I would point out is the fact that you two have had concern and caring for John and the desire to help him. This is God's love working through you. It's an example that it's real. For that's where it comes from. Your actions are living proof of God's love. I know that doesn't explain everything, but it's a start. Believe in God, believe the Bible, believe in eternity. It all comes in time."

***

"Man, you do get into some heavy stuff. Does that boggle your mind sometimes?"

"Sure. Kind of new experience – teaching others. You grow with it. Easy lessons first; hard ones later. Then you have to be tuned in with that special inner ear. You know?"

"A – yeah, I think so. Hey, can you believe this? There's Eddie and Wanda! Hey, Eddie. A – good to see ya. Hi Wanda."

"Oh good morning Mr. Davies. Hey, look out, church, here come the walls...."

"Right. Better stand back. Hey, a – Eddie, I'd like you and Wanda to meet Ann Davies – OOP – I mean...."

178

"Ann Davies!?!? Well, well, Paul. You try'un to tell us some'thun here ole buddy?"

"Ha – oh – Paul. Hello, Eddie and Wanda. Paul's told me about you, and well I guess my brand-new fiancé' has his own unique way of announcing our engagement. It is true, but right now I'm still Ann Winfield and very pleased to meet you."

"Pleased to meet you too, Ann. Eddie never tells me much, outside of golf scores. Nice to meet you in person. And Ann,, really great to hear about you and Paul. All the best wishes in the world."

"Thank you, Wanda. Nice to meet you in person too, maybe you and I could exchange a few secrets, huh? I never get much out of Paul except golf scores, either."

"Hey, Paul, what ya got us into here? Just kidd'un, Ann. Really, I'm pleased to meet you."

"Thank you Eddie. Same here."

"Well, shall we go in?"

After Church

"Well, you're right Paul. Didn't hurt a bit. A – kinda neat really. But, I thought, a, was that Pastor Brown?"

"No, he doesn't start until the first – couple more Sundays. You'll have to come back then."

"Oh, oh, there you go, you church people. See, you get us here one Sunday and then you...."

"Cool it. Won't hurt you to miss Sunday golf once in a while. You'd just get beat anyway."

"OK, OK, what do we do now?"

"Well, Paul what do you think? Shall we introduce them to Chuck's, or do you already know the place?"

"Chuck's? Chuck's? You hold'un out on us, Pauly babe. What gives?"

"It's a place I ran into by accident. Come on, I'll show you!"

Chuck's

"Hey, you *have* been hold'un out. Check the box!"
"Say Ann, this place does have a certain something, doesn't it?"
"I guess Paul and I think so. We've sure had some good times here."
"Now, if they just had a good shrimp salad...."
"As a matter of fact...."
"You're kidd'un!"
"Well, come on. First thing we got to do is – toast the 'to be's'."

A Good Sunday Night Was Had By All
Ann's House
(Later)

"Ah, well, Ann, Am tells me this is the big party night, huh?"
"I hope it's going to be big, or, successful. I've told the class, mostly girls, they could bring a friend. I hope I'm not asking for it. I have done that before. The idea of course, is to introduce new people to the group. I hope they don't tear up the place."
"Oh, we'll help you control them. We're used to big parties. Come from big families."
"OOPS, there's the door bell. Here we go."
"Hello."
"Paul! Hi, am I glad to see you. You can help me with the party."
"Yeah, I heard. Big shin-dig huh?"
"I don't really know. I told them they could bring a friend...I didn't say boy or girl...so I don't know. Oh, oh, was that the bell again? Guess so. Well here we go...again. Hello, girls. Come in. A, hi!"
"Mrs. Winfield...this is George and this is Tarrell."

"Hi guys, nice to meet you."

"Hi."

"Hi."

"And this is Evans, and this is Cole, and this is Nathan."

"Pleased to meet you. Come in, make yourselves at home. Come on down, we're going to have the party downstairs."

"Wow! Mrs. W, nice place you have here."

"You can drop the Mrs. I'm Ann and this is Paul and I think you know Pastor Brown and Mrs. Brown."

"Mrs. W, I mean Ann, a, nice music. Do you mind if we dance?"

"A, well, I....," glancing toward Pastor Brown.

"Let me answer that question, with Ann's permission, of course. If you're asking if it's OK in the presence of a pastor, the answer is: 'Sure!' When I was growing up we had family dances all the time. Right at home, live music and all. My Aunt Jenny taught me to dance. I danced with my sister, my mother, my aunts. My mother was the best dancer around – taught me a few moves. Dancing in itself isn't bad, it's how you do it. With Ann's permission again, I say go ahead – dance. But if you don't do it right in my opinion, I'm cutt'un in. I do have rhythm you know.

***

"Whew! Well, I guess that wasn't too bad – considering."

"Oh, I don't know, I only had four dances. I used to do better than that when I was dancing with my mother... Just kidd'un."

"Did you hear the jokes they were telling over there?"

"No. Maybe it's better I didn't"

"Oh no, the ones I heard anyway were definitely OK, like, 'Do you know what they said when the Red Sea parted?'"

"I give up, what?"

"Holy Moses! Or, 'What kind of music upset Goliath?'"

"OK, what?"

"Hard rock!"

"Ha ! Wow! I guess I missed all the good stuff."

"I guess I did, too. Well I think Am and I are going to retire. You two can sit up and enjoy the fire. Nice party. We'll see you for clean up in the morning."

"OK, ga' night. You know Ann, this was not the kind of party I'm used to, but that's good! Nobody insulted, nobody drank too much – neat. These kids – at least a generation gap away. But they were fun, you know?"

"I know."

"Something else I know. Although I do have trouble soak'un it all up. *I'm* different! I can't believe it, think'un back how I used to act and think – not long ago, and it's you. You made the difference."

"I'm glad."

"And, you know, now they got me say'un it. Anyway, you know, when I think about go'un back, I mean be'un like I was, it seems dumb. Like – I don't know what – mud pies and sandbox or something. I donno. Maybe I feel like, 'been there, done that and wised up'!"

"I do know and I *am* glad. I do so want you to feel and know the things that I do. About life I mean. It's so good and so real."

"I guess not long ago I would have laughed at that. You know? And all those crazy sayings we used to – well I guess people still do – laugh at, like, 'Life's a bitch and then you die!' And all that. Unfortunately, tragically, if you live in this asphalt jungle and let it be your whole life, then that's true. Sad!"

"Yes, it is!"

Chapter 11
Next Day

"Hello, Nina. Well, hello! What's up? You usually don't call me in the morning."

"Oh, Mom, I'm devastated! It's Neil! Ya, again. Can you come over? I can't explain it on the phone."

"Sure, are you all right? I mean physically?"

"Yes, yes he didn't beat me or I'm not sick or anything. I just, well can you come over for a while?"

"Sure, sure, give me a couple minutes to pick up a few things. I'll be right there."

"OK. See you."

Nina's

"Well, baby, what's happening? Must be important. Let me get a cup."

"Mom, I've told you part of it already. But, it's worse and it's to a point, well, I just have to do something..... Neil wants to get physical, and I know how you feel about that. But in the past, I gave in to him, because I was afraid I'd lose him. Now, it seems that's all that's important to him. Mom, I don't want to lose him, but I don't know what to do."

"Honey, I know that's a tough situation. I really do. But let's look at it. You do want Neil, and you do want a good life with him. You don't want to go a year or so and then the divorce scene and all. Right?"

"Yes, but...."

"How would you feel if you saw him with another woman, sometime after your married?"

"I'd die! But I'd kill him first!"

"Well, I'd hate to see that happen."

"I can't believe he'd do that."

"I can't either, Nina but you must have some deep down question in your mind or you wouldn't be so upset. Let's try to fix it. Now, not later."

"No, I don't... well, OK. So, maybe I do! I don't know. I just know I feel awful!"

"I know I've said this before, but think about it. Don't marry him... right now, and don't have sex with him. If he really loves you, he'll want to talk to you about it. Tell him how you feel. I think you're too smart to want to tie up with a guy for sex alone. If it's real, he'll come through this and if he doesn't, he's not the guy you want. And what you suffer now is not nearly what you would suffer later if it flopped. Trust me."

"Mom, that's easy for you to say, but it's not easy to live."

"I know."

"NO! You don't!"

"Yes, I do! And that's why I don't want you to find out the hard way, because I do know and I also know there's a much better way. Don't blow it! Nina, baby, I'm going to insist you promise me something or I'll – well you just do it. Look, you promise me you'll give it some more time. Back off from Neil. If it's real, he'll come to you. Just give it some time and talk to me again – later, OK?"

"I'll think about it."

"Well, do more than that!"

Paul's House
(Later)

"Hello, Nina – Nina is that you? What's the matter!? Wait a minute I can't understand. Ann's in the hospital? NO! No, oh, no. Wait a minute, wait a minute. She was in a car accident? She's at SW General - Nina you said she's critical – what? -

How critical? Oh no! I'm coming right over. I'm coming right over, OK? Take it easy, now. I'm come'un right over. All right, good bye."

Aw man - head-on coming down some hill out of Nina's - wherever that is - she's messed up inside and out - bad! Gotta get there!"

***

"Nina! Nina! Where is she?"

"In the back Paul. They won't let you in right now. There's a whole bunch of people there. Paul, it's bad! I'm scared!"

"I know Nina. Just hang on. Let's see what we can find out."

"They say they can't tell much right now. They're just trying to keep her alive. Paul! Neil, hold me!"

"I got you, honey, just hold on. I think it probably looks worse at first. Give 'um time to check her out and do what they have to do. It takes time. She's in the best place she could be. Come on, sit down, there's nothing we can do right now. They're doing everything possible. By the way, I'm Neil. Sorry we have to meet under such circumstances. Nina's told me about you – all good. Pleased to meet you."

"A, same here, Neil. Guess I'm a little shook, more than a little right now. Nina said – a head-on. What happened anyway?"

"She was going down that long hill coming from Nina's place, curve at the bottom. Some guy in a pickup didn't make the curve – was on her side of the road. And they hit – head-on!"

"What happened to him?"

"Hate to tell you this, but – he's dead."

"Oh, no."

"A , Honey somebody just came out from back there. Let me see if I can find out anything. Stay here with Paul. Just a sec...."

"Well, she said she's still unconscious, on the respirator and

IV's and of course they're taking x- rays. Can't tell too much, yet. She said we could wait in the room down the hall and she would let us know of her status as soon as she could."

(Hours Later)

"Hello Paul, anything new?"

"No, Neil she hasn't stirred. Hasn't even opened her eyes. Oh, one thing, they did say she has a skull fracture they are concerned about. I don't like it when they say they are concerned. Usually try to be positive. I don't like it when they say 'concerned'."

"Me either. Say Paul, you've been here for hours. No sleep, nothing to eat. You better take a break. Nina and I had some breakfast. Go get something. We'll be around."

"Oh, maybe later. I just couldn't handle it right now. Maybe later."

"Well, you know, she's resting and they've got everything going that's possible to do. This could take a while."

"I know. I – a – I just want to be here right now. Maybe later, maybe later, OK?"

"Sure."

"Oh, Paul, Pastor Brown and Amy are coming over, and they said they are praying for Ann and for you and Nina."

"Oh, OK."

***

"Aw, Pastor! Why do these things happen?" Why? Why her? Me, I could see. But she doesn't deserve it. She's always so good."

"Paul, you know what they say. 'The rain falls on the just and the unjust.' We're here with a free will and things just happen in this world. Good things – bad things. But, try to look on the positive side; she's getting the best of care, and she's in the hands of the Good Lord no matter what happens. Don't you feel assured when you know she's in the best hospital around and with the best medical staff? Well then, take it one step farther and be assured and comforted because she's in the hand of the Almighty, the Creator, that's the best there is. Rest easy, Paul and leave it to Him!"

"Thanks Pastor. I guess I know these things, but it's tough just the same. Here we sit. We just have to wait. We can't do anything. Shows you how really helpless you are I guess."

"I know, it's a tough lesson sometimes, Paul."

"You know, I been think'un. It, in a way, forces you to seek God. There's nothing else you can do. I can't go in there and offer these guys more money, or grab one of them by the collar and threaten to beat the - stuff'un out of him if he doesn't fix it now. There's nothing I can do. I been trying to connect up with the Lord awful hard since this happened. Before, it was – a – oh, nice thing to do or sump'thun. but now, it's serious – life or death. Aw, man I don't even like to say that. But it's serious – no games."

"I know Paul, these things do bring us to the Lord in a way we've never been brought before. I hesitate to say God does this intentionally. That seems an awful extreme measure. But I do know that it happens. And when that happens, open yourself up to Him. Receive Him, don't blame Him for the things that happen in this world. He's here to help us through it. He has a much better plan for us, beyond our understanding. Ask for His will to be done – His will. There's no better deal than that."

"I don't know if I'm ready for all that. I just want Ann back,"

"I know, Paul, I know."

Two Days Later

"Pastor, it isn't get'un any better, that thing in her head. They're still concerned.. 'Concerned!' I'm go'un out of *my* head. Where's God?"

187

"Paul, these things don't always go the way *we* think they should. They're doing everything they can and we're doing everything we can. Man, you realize you haven't changed your clothes in three days? You haven't had a good night's sleep, and I don't know what you've eaten. Paul, Amy's got a hot meal waiting for you at Ann's. Let me drive you over there. You get something to eat – take a rest. Clean up and come back this evening. Nina and Neil are coming in this afternoon. Say, man, you haven't even shaved. If Ann woke up and saw you now, you'd – well you'd want to look nice for her. Come on."

"OK."

Ann's House

"I tell you Am, I don't know when I've seen anybody worry so over anybody. Paul's going to do himself in."

"I'm afraid so. Oh oh, the phone. I'll get it."

***

"Hello, yes this is Amy. Paul's upstairs. I can – yes, Neil, yes. Oh, no, when? Oh, Neil I'm so sorry to hear that. Is Nina there? Is she OK? Yes...yes...yes... I'll tell Paul. Nina wants to stay there? Well, you take care of her. I know you will. Well, thank you Neil for calling and I'll tell Paul. He's sleeping. OK, I will! Bye."

"Oh, Andrew, that was Neil at the hospital. Ann died about 30 minutes ago."

"Yes, I gathered from your conversation. I sure hate to hear that."

"I do too, and I hate to have to wake Paul and tell him that."

"I'll do it, Am, I'll do it."

Chapter 12
Somewhere

"There is our Ann. (to the earth people) Did your mission go well? With Paul?

"Oh yes, I think so. I had forgotten how involved you can get, even making mistakes, while going through the physical part. And how much carries over. Yes, yes – Paul has come a long way, even though he doesn't think so. I think he will continue. He has realized and experienced enough of the truth that I don't think he will want to go back, even though I'm sure the tempter will work on him."

"And the Pastor – Brown?'

"As you can see, he's only beginning his work. He is rich in it, and will accomplish much!"

"I see you have established quite a deep connection yourself."

"Yes, Paul and I have. We call it the real thing, quite appropriate don't you think? Especially for something that is eternal. Paul and I have formed a union made of love. It is beautiful and will last forever."

"I know. Of course. And you're right, they are always beautiful – and lasting."

"I think I have to be with Paul right now. He is about to go through a very difficult period. He has to do it himself and make up his mind himself of course. But he does need my help."

"We are with you, Ann."

Ann is one of the Angels. Amy will be soon. Ann has helped Paul a great deal and Amy has helped Andrew get where he is. She is not one of them now, but she has been influenced by recent past generations, influence that she is not even aware of. It does carry over

Ann's House
Pastor Brown Wakes Paul - Jill's Visit

"Paul - Paul - sorry to disturb you - but I ...."

"It's all right. I know. Ann's gone, isn't she?"

"I'm afraid so, Paul. Sorry to have to tell you. She passed away a short time age. She never regained consciousness. Nina is with her. How did you know?"

"I donno, just did. It's accepting it I'm having trouble with. A – is everything OK? I mean, you say Nina is with her...?"

Everything's OK, that is, Nina's with Neil. And by the way Paul, Neil has certainly come through for Nina. He took off work and has been with her every minute."

"Good, maybe something good will come of this. I – I – aw – I don't even want to talk...."

"Why don't you just rest, Paul. There's nothing you can do now. I don't think you could see her if you went to the hospital. Just take it easy. You need it. I'll check on Nina and whatever else needs to be."

"I don't think I can sleep. I don't think I can do anything. Aw, Pastor, why? Why this? This is the end of everything. I..."

"Paul, why don't you let me give you something to make you sleep? You need it. Just relax."

"Oh, I don't care. I hope I don't wake up."

"You'll wake up and you'll feel better, later. Trust me. Paul, she's in very good hands right now. Believe it!"

"I don't know what I believe right now. You better give me something strong now, before I change my mind."

"OK, sit still."

***

"Nina, honey, I wish there was something I could do to help you. But I don't know. These things make you feel so bad, not only bad, but so darn helpless. I can't turn back the clock. I can't say anything to you that will really do any good. What can I do? If I knew, I'd do it."

"Neil, you've done more than you think. Just stay with me. You don't have to do anything. Just stay with me. Stay close!"

"That I can do, honey. That I can do."

Ann's House Again

"Oh hello Nina – Neil, come in. Nina, you have our sincerest sympathy. Ann's a wonderful person and we all will miss her very much. Please sit down. Is there anything I can get you? Coffee?"

"Thank you, Pastor. Is Paul here?"

"Yes, he's upstairs. Was sleeping, but I thought I heard him moving around. Just a minute, I'll see. A, Nina, we feel out of place here in Ann's house. Is there anything we can do?"

"Pastor, you just stay right here. I'm sure Mom would want you to, and I do too. Don't worry about it. And it's nice to have you and Mrs. Brown around right now. You just stay put."

"Well, thank you Nina. Oh, hello, Paul. How you feeling? Get a rest?"

"Yeah, sure, better. Oh, Neil – Nina. I'm sorry. Is everything OK? I mean..."

"Yes, Paul. I just – well I'm OK. I do have a special message for you. It's from Jill. You know her? She said she was in Mom's Sunday school class and she met you. Her aunt works at the hospital and called to tell her about Mom. She came to the hospital and wanted to talk to you. She said she didn't know Mom had a daughter, but when she found out, she addressed her message to me, also. But it was originally intended for you. She said she wanted to tell you what a friend told her when her mother died. She said the friend told her three things. First, remember that this is just a temporary parting. Second, she is in a better place. And third, it's true! She said it made her feel better. It made me cry. I thanked her very much... Neil..."

"It's OK, honey, go ahead and cry, it'll make you feel better."

"A – thanks Nina. Yeah, I remember Jill. That's neat. Good way to look at it, I guess. I still feel rotten. I don't know if it makes you feel better or not, but I guess I've got some of it to do, too."

At the Funeral

Aw - man - I hate this. Why does it always have to rain at funerals. Pastor said some nice words about Ann at church. Tore me up. I wonder how Nina handled it? I don't think she'd make it if she didn't have Neil's broad shoulders to cry on. Good thing - I guess. Hey, he doesn't seem like such a bad guy. Nobody said he was a bad guy. I guess.

Aw - here it comes. She's in there. They're go'un to put it in the ground. Aw man - I don't know - I - what? That's her Sunday school class, and that's Jill! She's going to stand next to me! She wants to hold my hand - she is! Man - can you believe how much meaning can be in a little hand squeeze! From a little girl!

"...ashes to ashes... dust to dust. What was ashes before will be again, but what lives inside will live forever, Amen."

That ashes thing gets me - but I guess what I knew - still do - is what lived inside. Pastor says that part is still alive somewhere. I don't know where. But I do know I still love her. I'll always love her - always!"

"Oh, hi Jill, thanks for coming, and thanks for that message. I appreciate it."

"You're welcome Mr. Davies. Bye bye."

"Bye bye."

Bye bye? Hum - hum - .

Going Home

"Paul, I know there's not much anybody can say right now that will ease the hurt a great deal.

"Now is a time when you look to your faith and a time when your faith will help you through. I also know you have had some messages from people concerning this, at church, from friends etc. You know how deeply you feel for Ann. Something like nothing else, and that hasn't died, has it? Even though Ann is gone.

"When I was a boy people told me about heaven with gold paved streets and running with milk and honey. I didn't believe it even then. I don't think heaven has streets. But whatever, wherever it is, I think we get a clue about it through the real feeling we have for one another. The real good genuine feeling you had and I'm sure still have for Ann, I believe is a clue as to what heaven is all about. And I think it's true evidence that it exists. Keep her in you heart, and believe me, you'll see her again!"

"Yeah, I hope your right Pastor. I guess it all has to soak in a little. Thank you, anyway."

Next Sunday
Church

"Morning Pastor."

"Morning, Paul. What are you doing here so early?"

"Just still trying to sweep some of the cob webs out, I guess, Pastor. I have been sitting in with Ann in her class for a while. I think it has just become a habit. Those kids got to me a bit, maybe more than a bit."

"I think I know what you mean."

"Pastor, let me tell you right out what I'm thinking about. Would it be possible for me to take Ann's class? I know I'm not trained or anything but – well, I just can't get it out of my head.

Those kids and all, I just don't want it to end for me. I know those girls know more than I do. But I just want to – well, I just want to be with them and do what I can."

"Paul, old Mrs. Allen agreed to fill in till we get a full time teacher. She's 77. I know she will be glad to let someone else take over. Let me tell you something – teaching is 90% desire and 10% training. You tell me you have the 90%. I'll see to it you get the other 10."

"Pastor, you got a deal."

Another Sunday

"Morning Pastor."

"Morning Paul. How's things going currently?"

"Strange you should ask. I been thinking...."

"Um, that's my line. 'Bout what?"

"Well, been think'un 'bout what you told me before. I guess I'm one of those people who thought he had it all figured out, small things anyway. You know, I could dope the horses, beat the IRS, and get it wholesale. But I missed the big one. Couldn't see the forest for the trees."

"Yes. Been there...."

"Hey, now, *that's* my line. Aw, just kid'un. Seriously though, Pastor I *do* feel like I'm one of those guys who's out smarted himself. Ann tried to get to me enough times. You did too, I guess. For a smart guy I was awfully slow catch'un on. You know she's been gone a while now and yet I still love her. Seems like just as much as I ever did. Kinda brings it home to me that the 'real thing' that we almost joked about *is* real. Don't know why it took something like this to make me see it. And then, Pastor you know – Ann. I can't help but feel there's something about her. If I didn't know better, I'd think – well, like she was sent here or something. Aw, I don't know. That's crazy. But, well you ever have any feelings like that?"

"Yes, I think I know what you mean. It is kinda strange. I

guess it makes me think about that line in the Bible, 'entertained angels unaware.'"[33] 'Course nobody knows for sure I guess, but, yes, true. Makes you wonder!"

"Ya does. And something else, really important and what I didn't get, is that our relation with God and the church and all is like that – same thing. Not surface and physical but, well, what can I say, 'real'! Is that what they mean by 'seeing the light'?"

"Thought about that, too. Know what? I think the answer is - yes!"

---

[2] Heb 13:2 King James Ver.

Chapter 13
Church

Five Years Later

"Thank you. everyone for coming today. We're here to dedicate not one but two additions to our church. I for one find this wonderfully unbelievable. Five years ago, I remember trying to decide whether to accept Pastor Brown as our pastor. I confess I had some doubts. I'm happy to say those doubts have been erased and because of the enthusiastic and tireless work of *our pastor*, Pastor Andrew Brown, we are here today dedicating a new addition to our church – necessary to house the growth in the last five years.

Also we are more than pleased to dedicate at the same time, the new education building. And I would be amiss if I did not recognize that it is possible in a great part due to the faithful work and energies put forth by our chairmen of the Education Committee, Mr. Paul Davies.

The building committee has given me two plaques, one reading 'Andrew Brown Wing' and the other, 'Paul Davies Hall.' They will be attached above the doors on each of the new additions to remind us of the work and dedication of these two outstanding members of our congregation."

***

"Thank you, George for all the good words. You know if you didn't have that already made, I would insist it read 'Ann Winfield Hall.' It is she who inspired it all."

"Yes, I remember Ann very well."

"Well, Eddie, what a day huh?"

"Yeah, I thought it was something to see you welcome Neil and Nina's little guy in Sunday school. Man, time flies, huh?"

"Sure does, sure does... Well what ya say, Glick, you and Wanda want to go out to Chuck's and relax?"

"Hey, sounds great! Let's do it!"

Chuck's

"Hum, been doing this a long time, you know?"

"Yeah! Hey Paul, you OK?"

"Paul! Paul! What's the matter?"

Special Angel

"Paul."

***

"Oh nothing, no, not a thing. It's just that music, this place, and all that's happened... I – I just wasn't by myself there for a minute. No, I sure wasn't – and it was great!"

Much Later

"Ah, the beauties of this world are a wonderful thing to observe."

"Yes, they certainly are. I have noticed the union of our Ann and Paul, and the Browns, whom we observed on earth some time ago, that is, many revolutions of their planet ago. That time of course is meaningless here. But what a beautiful thing it has become. And it all started during their earth experience, and is still growing, even after expanding to the wonderful position it is now. Their earth growth and their acceptance of greater things there has given them their start here. Their love has out lasted the trivial problems they had on earth so long ago. Strange how people going through earth experience seem so saddened – even destroyed emotionally by some event in the earth time. But that is the way it must be. So the earth experience will seem real at the time."

"Speaking of their time, how long has that been?"

"Not long really, by their planet's revolutions as you say, 982+27 of their years."

"Oh, nothing really, considering – it will last for eternity. What a wonderful thing has been created."

"It certainly has!"

***

"And a couple of those bales of hay could have changed it all!"

"I know. I know."

THE END